Guilty

PAM BRIDY

authorHOUSE®

AuthorHouse™
1663 Liberty Drive
Bloomington, IN 47403
www.authorhouse.com
Phone: 1 (800) 839-8640

Published by AuthorHouse   07/17/2015

ISBN: 978-1-5049-2286-9 (sc)
ISBN: 978-1-5049-2285-2 (e)

Print information available on the last page.

This book is printed on acid-free paper.

Contents

The Prologue

March 9, 2007

As the nursing assistants entered the operating room, they were stunned to see Mr. Tunnel back so soon. They were wondering what had happened and what kind of surgery they were performing on him today. They had already done two heart by-passes on him about six weeks ago. They thought everything was functioning as it should be. At least during the last operation things went smoothly.

Dr. Sampson walked in and said" Ladies we need to do another by pass on Mr. Tunnel." They all looked at each other as to say didn't you check everything the first time?

"Now, lets get started." "This was unexpected so we need to put a rush on his procedure." (why because it blows your schedule with what you had planned for today, or did you screw up and forget to check everything the last time?)

I know we have emergencies, but he acted like this was not suppose to happen and he was a little upset. Well, let's say he was quite upset. A repeat surgery within six weeks in between is not his cup of tea. "Okay ladies, lets get started and get in and out ASAP."

All of a sudden we heard all the bells and whistles going off and Dr. Sampson screaming "Alright, I want everyone to stop working. No one here will leave this room talking about what just happened." "Don't say anything or you be terminated immediately, plus will wish they never worked here." "Besides I know a lot of people in the area if someone decides to leave." "This is not a problem, I will make it go away and you will have nothing to worry about as long as my group keeps quiet." "It' just unfortunate that Mr. Sampson passed away on the table."(what is he talking about)

We were a group of ten that were handpicked by him. Although he had six of us working here today. There were five scheduled but then I got paged to help. Talk about this will never leave this room, he didn't have to tell me that. There was no way I was going to say anything threat or no threat he was right. Most of the time there were five of us that worked together, he also hand picked the ones he wanted for each case. I wasn't on the list. Most of the time I was always picked. Of course, today was my unlucky day. He meant what he said and what happened will be forgotten because he was the head of the department. No one will ever go above him on anything. Everyone was looking at each other and thinking the same thing. After this mess I was heading home.

Chapter 1

Greyson General was world famous for cardiology. Any where from treating heart issues to operating on them, to doing transplants. They started slow and began to rise on the list to became one of the highest rated heart treatment centers in the United States. Dr. Sampson was proud of what he accomplished. They built buildings for research with donations coming in at a high rate, it seemed like the buildings went up faster than the hospital could keep up with them.

The group of ten really liked working for Greyson General It was set on a beautiful location in the suburbs of Chicago. They purchased a large plot of land, thinking far ahead into the future, however, the future came faster than they could keep up with the growth. Now they have five buildings and the rumor was they were putting a wing on just for children. It was a beautiful hospital with many additions added on over the years. It seemed like they were always doing something to make the hospital better. The OR was just rebuilt all over again and we finally had a new lounge/sleeping room to go too.

Greyson General was set close to Michigan Lake with plenty of room for expansion which they seem to be doing regularly. It was built at a time when land was freely available. Chicago was just starting to blossom. There was an old part of Chicago and a newer one that was growing. Many years ago, a lot of the old houses had been torn down and the hospital decided to purchase as much land as possible. It was beautiful with many windows looking out over Michigan Lake. It wasn't directly in the city, but close enough for the Emergency Room to be getting quite busy. It seemed the city was growing out to meet the hospital. They put a running path entirely around the faculty for employees who wanted to exercise plus they had an exercise room down stairs for employees who wanted to work out, during their lunch time. They even had showers there for employees to use before returning to work. It was becoming quite the facility to work at.

The apartments and townhouses around the hospital were going up around the facility as fast as the hospital was expanding and being rented or being bought just as fast. Some buildings had waiting lists. They were quaint little apartments and office buildings that lawyers, doctors and nursing staff would be interested in buying. That's how Jane got her apartment.

Chapter 2

It was Tuesday and I knew I was going to be in the operating room this AM. It was a beautiful and spring was finally here. It had been a long winter, especially since it started at the end of october. I decided to wear one of my spring outfits. My apartment looked beautiful. I had just bought some violets that I sat on the window sill of my living room. The ferns were in full bloom in the corner. I loved this place. It had windows wrapped around the corner of one side, with a porch to walk out onto. I spent many a day just sitting out there reading my favorite books, but now I don't have much time to do that anymore. I seemed to be working all the time. I looked out the window across from my apartment at my favorite coffee shop. I always stopped there every day to get a bagel and coffee.

But this morning I almost couldn't believe my eyes, Sam was across the street sitting outside at table in front of the coffee shop.

I had to hurry, fix my hair put make-up on which, I never wear to work. I tried to dodge the on coming traffic running across the street. "Sam, Sam" he looked over and saw me waving my hand. He raised his arm and motion for me to come over. I went over and gave him a big hug. "I was so worried about you".

"So, how are you?" "I'm good." "I've been gone for about a month now. I just had to leave town for awhile Jane." "That case really hit me hard." "I really thought that I had everything in order."

"That woman was butchered Jane." "The doctor really botched up that C-Section with her, to the point she now can not have any more children plus, that baby died and I could not do a damn thing more during the trial to win."

"I keep trying that court case over and over in my mind and I still can't seem to come up with anything I would have done differently." "My heart goes out to that family." "That doctor sure did have a hell of a group of defense attorneys, Barney and Associates, and they turned everything around, to the point that, it seemed like it was my clients fault." "That she did something wrong to cause her illness that caused her to have a C-section." "I could not break any of their experts on the list."

God, I was so mad and hurt." "I felt like this was my first case." "I prepared for this case a long time, but it didn't seem to matter, I mean this wasn't my first rodeo." "I have won plenty of cases for people and have won for people who have less injuries."

"Damn it, he cut right through her uterus and discovered she had massive fibroids which caused her to start to bleed out and cut the oxygen from the baby. The blood flooded her uterus so fast it basicly drowned the baby."

4

"So he says he had to make a decision of saving the baby or the mother." "I know that was a lie, sympathy for him, yea right, he could of saved both, however he obsessively never ran into that problem before and by the time he called for a surgeon, it was such a mess, it was to late." "So their decision was to rip her from having anymore children." "He should of caught it with a sonogram."

"She kept telling him she had a lot of pain and he wrote it off as braxton hicks." "I hurt so much for her." "I felt so bad, I could of cried, and then my client told me I did great and she couldn't have found a better lawyer."

She said she was alright with the decision. "Jane how would you feel when you just lost a case and your client tells you I was a good lawyer and she was not angry." "I was hurt, pissed off and at the same time I was trying not to break down and cry." "I know, I could see it on your face." Jane said. "I just thought it was a good idea to take some time off." "I just had to get away" "I left my apartment go but I kept my office" "In fact I told Phyliss just to go in and open the mail, pay the bills and that was all the time I wanted her to spend in the office." "She practically got up and kissed me." "I think I made her day." "I had her going in circles."

SAM

As a young boy, Sam often went to the creek with his best friends to go swimming. The old swimming hole was a popular place for the kids of Gordon, Alabama. Gordon was a small town in which everyone knew everyone. A place where you would want your children to grow up in. The usual white picket fences and beautiful streets lined with large oak trees which all lead to town square. Sam loved his town, but always told his best friends Frank and Kerry that he was no matter what, moving away from Gordon. He wanted to explore other great cities. So Sam's studies always came first. He felt the only way to do what he wanted, was to study hard and get into college.

Sam never seemed stuck on himself, although all the girls in Gordon thought he was probably the most handsome boy in school. He grew into an intelligent and very handsome man even though he was oblivious, to what girls were saying because he kept his head in the books. He didn't even go to his prom, which broke his mom's heart, but this is where he was different, he wanted to make it into college and have an opportunity to find himself, not that he didn't love Gordon, but he just wanted more. He never thought of himself as handsome, in fact he considered himself a nerd.

Sam, Frank, and Kerry graduated and all decided to go to the same college, Penn State University. For Sam it was what he always wanted and he was glad that Frank and Kerry were coming along. Penn State had a great solid law college. Frank still didn't know what he wanted to do yet and probably wouldn't until he was there awhile, so he probably would go in undecided.

Sam had matured into a man with a well toned body and deep blue eyes. He also had a beautiful thick head of light brown hair with a hint of gray running through it.

After graduating college, he decided to go to Chicago to open a law firm. It was a big city, and offered you just about anything you wanted. Gordon was his home but Chicago was his future. Now at the age of 29 it's as if he never changed. However, his hair had a little more gray running thru it which he hated. Sam's inheritance of gray hair did not make him feel young. Sometimes when he looks into the mirror he curses his father's genes. His father started to show gray hair earlier in life than Sam and just decided he had to live with it.

Sam was a planner, and gray hair wasn't one of them, but he didn't want to dye his hair so he just decided to forget about it. He had no idea how many women thought his partly gray hair made him look so distinguished looking. Sam always knew where he was going even from week to week. He even planned ahead for weekends. He always left his secretary know where he was and his phone was on. He wanted to be there for his clients or if something new came up, Sam was differently a planner. Phyliss was his secretary and she could repeat his goodbye's without even hearing it. She had been his secretary for 5 years now and he loved her like an aunt. "See you Monday Phyliss, my phone is on and I will be available anytime no matter where I am."

He liked to know exactly what had to do be done in the office when he arrived down to where he wanted to have dinner that night if he had to stay at the office. Phyliss and Sam worked well together and he felt so lucky when she applied for the job. She knew what he wanted before he had to ask for it. This was just what he needed. He never took advantage of his appearance to get women, although most women would die to sink there claws into him. However, Sam was oblivious to it all.

He was dedicated to his clients. He loved what he did. It started in college and even to his journey of setting up his own law office. He was an honest man that anyone could tell as soon as they met him and they did.

Soon, by word of mouth his cases started coming in at a fast pace. Sam was so much into his work, he forgot about the dating scene. This was the one thing his mother pounded into him. Be polite and always make a woman feel important. He was one of those rare men that most women dreamed about, but never could find or had the opportunity to catch. He never cared about being handsome. He took his college years very seriously.

Sam and his roommates Frank and Kerry got along great. Even though Sam was always cracking down on the books and that was his priority, it didn't mean Frank or Kerry did the same thing.

Chapter 3

Sam was so happy when he found an old house along Michigan Avenue that had been placed on the market for sale. As soon as he walked in he knew this place was going to be his second home. The first floor had beautiful hard wood floors with old fashion floor to ceiling windows across the entire front of the house.

He decided to make his office on the second floor and tore down one wall to enlarge the room. He made the entire second floor his office.

He had given Phyliss his assistant a budget and she was very good in keeping below it. She treated me like her nephew. He wanted a place where his clients could be comfortable sitting on a sofa or chair while discussing their case. It reminded him of a small living area away from his desk and phones. His office was almost entirely done in Dark Mahogany. Phyliss always knew never to disturb him when he was with a client unless if was an emergency.

Downstairs he designed a beautiful office for Phyliss his assistant and he also designed a large library where he knew he would be spending most of his time even though his office was larger. The library had books from top to bottom. Sam did a lot of reading when he was in college. So besides his personal reading which was mostly cases and then he had all his law books he acquired during his college years which he referred to frequently. Most of his books were regarding medical malpractice cases that he referred back to. Sam wasn't one for extravagance or showing off his wealth. He was one that cared about all his clients equally no matter how much he was charging them. Phyllis put the woman's touch to the office purchasing everything that was needed to make a beautiful office. Sam would never give this office up. This was his home more than his home was.

Chapter 4

Jane said "So you do still have your office." "You know I couldn't let my office go." "When I decided to go to the Bahamas it was beautiful there." "I went scuba diving, which I never did before." "It was great." "I think I ate everything I could get my hands on." "I had not eaten much when I was preparing for the case."

"My beach hut as they call them was wonderful." "It literally was right on the beach." "I really could of lived there for months, without even thinking about Chicago."

"While I was on my R & R, Phyliss sent me this letter, and wrote in the corner I KNOW (in big letters), you will really be interested in this one, since your friend works at the hospital." "I thought this would get your curiosity going while your away." "It will give you something to think about while you are gone." "Let me know so I can get started if you are going to reopen it." "I really want you to take this case."

"The letter was from Mrs. Tunnel, stating she feels there was more to her husband's death than what came out in court." "She asked if I would review the case and consider reopening it." "She felt that it was very important and she knew I wanted to know the truth as much as my client." "Phyliss knows me so well." "So I cut my vacation short because it was really on my mind and I wanted to get started on it as soon as possible." "So now I'm back, working my ass off, once again."

"Do you want to know the odd thing about it?" He said "What?" "Phyliss was in the office at her desk and was sitting there ready for work, had made coffee, pulled files, had done research and had tentative appointments set up and was just waiting for me to return, which I did 10 days early." "Boy, she knows me like a book, we work well together and I still don't know how lucky I was to get her."

"Now I have this case I'm going to reopen and have been working on it." "In fact, it has to do with one of the doctors in the hospital you work at." "Oh yea? Who" said Jane. "Now Jane you know I can't revel my clients or the defendant that a case was filed against." "Well I tried." she started laughing.

"Well, I know you are an excellent attorney and with out a doubt will put everything you have into this case." "You're damn straight I will." I said. "After the last one this one I will win no matter what".

"Well, are you going to be staying in the apartment where you did?" "No, I let my apartment go, so I found another one about three blocks closer to my office, it's pretty nice." "It has a great view of Michigan Lake from my living room." "It also has a great deck off the living room."

"In the summer it will be great to sit out there in the evening or weekends." "I don't know why I am saying that because I seem to live at the office when I am working on a case." "I really would like to break that habit and spend more quite days at home but I probably won't."

"When I came home from my so called sabbatical I did get a beer and went out and relaxed on the deck." "Looking at the lake and stars at night is something I never had the opportunity to do in my old place." "I was thinking of looking for a house."

"My place isn't beautiful according to a woman but I love it." "It's built like a log cabin on the lake." "It has a loft where my bedroom is and you can look down into the living room." "It has a Hugh fireplace that literately lights up the entire living room." "I love it." "It's just big enough for me." "Don't need much cleaning that's for sure." "Looking out over that lake in the evenings were beautiful." "I couldn't tell you how many times I sat there and watched the sunset." "I want to find something near here with the same setup only with a little bit of a woman's touch." "But, that's not now, and of course I want it bigger, however that's later." Now I am ready to get back to work." "No time for house hunting right now."

Jane said "Well, I am so glad I saw you." "I was so worried about you." "I moved also, I live right across the street". "It's much closer to work". "It's larger then I need but that's OK". "Well I better be going. I am so glad I saw you" said Jane "Give me a call sometime if you can (which I hope you will) my number is the same." "I will, talk to you later." (My heart was in my throat), it would be so nice to see him again, Jane thought. The last case hit him so hard. He worked like he had never worked before.

Chapter 5

The next night as she look out the window at the beautiful sunset, she was wondering who this claim was filed against. It would be nice if it was the doctor I work for. That man is a butcher and we all know it. I wish he didn't think he was as perfect as he thought he was. Well actually he is not perfect, is he? He has a conceit about him that some doctors have. Like they are untouchable. Well, maybe if Sam is reopening his case again he isn't going to be untouchable much longer.

Well I really can't think about that, I'm surprised I even have the time to sit down and think about anything. When I went back into the nursing lounge I sat down and started thinking about the previous case.

It was over a year ago and she hasn't thought about it much since it happened. If this is the doctor and Sam's case, I don't know what I will do. I never thought it would catch up with me, but since she had finally fallen in love with him and knew that when he left Chicago she didn't know where or how to begin to tell him if this is the case. Jane let's wait and see how it plays out.

Chapter 6

It seems so long ago, but actually it was just fourteen months ago today that the incident happened. We had a wonderful relationship, when we met. We laugh at each other and made love morning, noon and night. It was a romance that was meant to be, he caressed my body ever so softly it seemed like it would never stop or I never wanted him to stop. Our love making was something that I thought I would never receive from a man. Sometimes we would have campaign and strawberries in bed after we finished making love.

Everything was perfect. I was so much in love with him, I felt we were going to make a future with each other. But then the new case came up. I never asked him about the new case, but that night, he was so comfortable with me, he talked to me like I was his wife and he was going over the facts with me as if this was a normal conversation.

I didn't really say anything, except I told myself I had to leave. I couldn't bare seeing him tearing himself up anymore, knowing what I knew and he didn't.

At first I was telling him I had to work when we were suppose to be going out. Then I made an excuse that I had to go home to California for a weekend.

One of my grandparents was in the hospital, that lasted about a week. Once I told him I had to go out of town for classes for my job. He began to start wondering if I was making excuses not to see him or if all of a sudden things were really happening to fast.

I kept a low key about his case and at the same time trying to keep our relationship some what serious. Then it happened, one day, I was giving him another one of my excuses and he asked me to sit down.

He said, "Jane, I think the little time we are now spending together is not helping us at all. "We seen to be drifting away." "Not because of my feelings, not because I don't feel I am falling out of love with you, but with your work and me trying to get ready for this case, I think we should give ourselves a break."

I said to myself (Oh my gosh it worked) I felt so bad but I had to do it. I didn't want to loose my job, because Sampson was still my boss.

"Sam I am so sorry. I truly am falling in love with you also, but I understand". "Just keep in touch with me and let me know how things are going." "Sometimes it helps to talk to someone who isn't working directly with the case and you can bounce things off of someone else." "We'll have to see how everything works." As time went on Sam really got busy and I hardly saw him at all.

Chapter 7

It was a cold but sunny day, walking down the sidewalk in Chicago going to work, when things transpired two years ago, I saw Sam walking across the street, it seemed that we both looked at each other at the same time. It seemed like it was meant to be. We just stood there and looked at each other for a few seconds and than before I knew it he was beside me.

He said, "Hi, my name is Sam", (of course he was gorgeous) I thought it seemed like an hour went by before I said anything, but it wasn't, I said "Hi my name is Jane, nice to meet you." We walked for what seemed like forever before anyone said anything but of course it wasn't.

Sam said "So where are you headed?" "To that building right up the street. Well then I guess we are heading for the same place. "I will be here for awhile, I have several individuals I need to talk to." "Well, then I guess I will be seeing you once and awhile, although it's a big place". "Your right about that." "Maybe I'll see you at lunch some time, we have a nice cafeteria and believe it or not the food is pretty good."

"What floor are you going to?" said Jane "Ten." said Sam "That's a pretty important floor". Sam said, "Well if it's your first time, your might as well start at the top." "Okay, well this is where I get off." said Jane. "Nice talking to you." Sam looked at his watch and Jane said "Oh are you just starting to work here?" (thinking he was a new doctor going up for his interview) "No, I have an appointment with one of your employees, have a good day"

So that is how it began. We started running into each other more frequently and sometimes we ate at the hospital cafeteria until he finally decided to ask me out. It seemed like pure heaven when I met Sam. We went for long walks. Had lunches together out side the cafeteria once in a while we had dinners.

Yesterday I saw Sam walking toward the hospital and he cross the street. "How about going to Sundown's right down the street tonight?" "I have an appointment with the hospital?" "What time is it for? "The appointment is for three o'clock, how about I pick you up about Eight o'clock?" "Good I said, I will see you then." "It's been great seeing you."

Sundown's was a restaurant, we ate at a lot. The waiter was happy to see us. "Hi Marcelo, how are you". "It's a miracle!, I thought you two broke up and went your separate ways." said Marcelo. "No, we just have a lot of business on our plate and we have taken a break." "Marcelo, I have to admit that this man, missed his girl a lot so I just had to see her." I laughed. "What a nice compliment or are you buttering me up for some information?" "No, I am telling the truth."

As we walked to his apartment, I said "Are we going up so I can see that beautiful view that you have been talking about? "Sure do you want to come up for a night cap also?" "Sure." He went to the bar and poured me a glass of Sherry and himself Scotch.

We were sitting on the deck when I said "This is beautiful. "You were right about the view, I don't think I ever saw it this high up." "Yea, I told you." "Someday I want to be able to enjoy this more often." "You should see the beautiful ships and sail boats that go by on weekends in the summer." "Some people have a lot of money, that's for sure."

"Boy, I have been so busy." said Jane. "It just seems Dr. Sampson is working us to death." "What do you mean?" said Sam. "Well it's just, that he's practically working us round the clock." "How long has that been going on?" "About nine months." (Well Jane when are you going to speak up? I think I will see how his case goes first.) Well, he will figure it out, I hope. I have to get away from this conversation.

We had a wonderful time that night. We laughed and reminisced about the times we had before his last trial. About the Sunday mornings in bed and the our love making. Jane said "You know, I have never enjoyed making love more with a man than I did with you." "We also have found a lot ways to take a shower than most couples." (he laughed) "Yea you're right" "I really enjoyed them myself." "Well we will have to start doing all of that again." said Sam.

"Sam, when this next trial is over do you think we might be able to start again and maybe this time make it." He grabbed me in his arms and held me tight. "Yes he said, Yes". "Jane I love you very much and if you think I am going to loose you, your crazy." "Oh Sam I love you so much too." "Let's hope this trial isn't to long and we can get back to working on our relationship."

We had a delicious meal, the wine was fantastic and we ended up exactly where I hoped we would. We had champagne and strawberries in bed and than made love all night. The love was something I never experienced before. It was as if it was meant to be. We just could not keep our hands off each other. His gentleness was far beyond anything I ever experienced with a man. We spent Sunday in bed making love all over again. It felt like we were trying to make up for time lost. Everything was just like before. We took a shower together and called and ordered breakfast to be delivered.

After we ate we went out for a walk. We walked and talked a lot, it seemed like we had never been a way from each other at all. Sam said he was the happiest when we started seeing each other. I was so glad to hear that, except for the heavy weight on my shoulders. I still wanted to wait until he went to trial to see how things were going to see if he was going to win the case or if he needed me. (I had a feeling he was going to need me to clinch the case.)

Chapter 8

"So tell me, how did you get mixed up with the wonderful Dr. Sampson?"

"He's worked with a lot of nurses, but I guess we stood out more than the rest to him." "He paged us one day to his office, ten of us" "He started his group of nurses about a year and a half ago." "When he became Chief Surgeon of Cardiology, he felt no one could object to what he wanted, after all he was in charge of all of us and the doctors."

"We all looked at each other and wondered why ten nurses were standing in front of the Chief Surgeon of Cardiology at the same time." "Well after all he was in charge of all of us and the doctors, residents and interns." "We all stood there and started laughing, because we all couldn't be fired at the same time."

Then Dr. Sampson came in and it was all quite again. He side "Ladies, I have worked with lots of nurses over the years here at Greyson General Hospital and have thought about all the nurses that worked for me." "We all looked at each other, he then continued." "I have reduced my list down to ten." "I want you to be my Nursing Assistance Group for Cardiology Surgery."

22

You young nurses are to me the best of the best." "Sure I am in charge and I really can do what I want however I did bring this to the attention of the board and they approved it, so no one has to worry about this new promotion." "You will get a sizable raise for this." "There will be long hours and hard work however the way I have seen you work, I feel the ten of you, will have no problems." I will have five working and five off." "That will be your rotation" "You will wear pagers twenty-four seven, when I need you in the OR I will page you." "It will be rough at first, getting use to your new schedules, however you will get into the swing of things." "I told the ER I will be taking all emergency operations, when necessary." "Your young, I know you will have no problems with keeping up with the schedule or me."

"If this proves to be a great success, which I hope it to be, you will get another substantial raise next year" "I have to see if I picked the right ones and if my idea will work." "It took along time to pick the ten of you but I think I have made a good choice.". "Your excused." "Oh and if someone does not care to take on this challenge, please see me within the week."

"Oh are there any questions." "Sir if you please." "Yes Jane." "Will we be getting any days off? "Yes, I won't be working Sundays, and everyone will be getting one weekend off a month unless I personally want you to assist on a particular operation."

After we left, we went back into our room and we just stood there. It was pretty amazing, his little speech, however it sounder like a lot of work. Trudy said "Well I'll, be willing to try it, even if it was just for the money."

"But if it's too much, money or no money I'll drop out." "I personally don't know how he will keep up with the surgeries. He said there will be four to five on and five off for a break, but to stay here in case he needs another one." "I just don't know how he is going to do it all." "We'll, we will see what takes place." "I'll try anything once, especially with an additional raise said Jane." I know Jane, the money does sound promising.

"And that is how it started." It's been a real roller coaster ride, that is for sure." "Sometimes we are so tired, we don't know which end is up." "But we are hanging in there." "It seems he his doing more and more operations every week."

"Oh and then he said "If you are wondering how I can do this, I am the head of the department". "Don't worry you will be well compensated for your work and availability." "I had no problem getting you an additional Thirty thousand dollars a year." "Any questions?"

"We all said no practically at the same time." "I think we were all in shock." "What could you say when something like that was just thrown at you?" "I could of quit the team, however if I did I think I would have been quitting my job also."

He than said "OKAY, I think you should either go back to the nurses lounge and get some sleep or go and eat, because you never know when your pager will go off."

"That's how it started and that is how it has been since then." "Well that's the story and here's my pager." "I'm glued to it seven-twenty four, it has become one of my body parts."

"Don't you think that is a little weird?" "That is so crazy." said Sam. "Yea, but what am I going to do about it?"

He's the head honcho, what he says goes and don't forget I DID get a Thirty thousand dollars raise out of it, although now that I have been working for awhile I don't think the money has made much of a difference." "Maybe Fifty thousand dollars, would have made it worth it now." "After we had our interview, well what he called an interview, we all went back to the lounge and plopped on anything that was available." "Can you imagine the gull of that man." said Trudy "He didn't even ask, he just took." "Yea, so what if he got us a raise, I don't want to be under his thumb and having to stop what ever I might be doing." Mary said "You mean sex, don't you?" Everyone started laughing, Trudy said "Don't be so nosy." "So that's how this miserable game of his started."

Chapter 9

We seemed to be working almost 24 hours a day for the last six months. I was exhausted. I no sooner be done with an operation, go back to the nurses lounge to take a nap or at least rest or try and eat something when my pager would go off, to get ready for another operation.

He even took all emergency surgeries that pertained to his specialty. Even if another doctor was treating the patient in the emergency room, and he found out the patient needed surgery Dr. Sampson told the other doctor he would take the surgery. He almost knew all the time when we got emergency patients in that needed surgery. Like he had a spy in the emergency room. He was walking around like he had the world on his shoulders. Not one administrative employee said anything. It was as if they were being paid to back off on all complaints.

We became known has the elite ten around the hospital. We all said if the other nurses think that, we would gladly exchange places in a second. The group of ten after about 3 months were finally all together one day. We could not believe it.

It was like a little party of sorority girls who haven't seen each other in years. Sounds stupid but we knew he was working us like dogs. After five pagers went off again and the other nursing assistants left, the rest of us started talking about what was going on all of sudden with Dr. Sampson. Jane said "Yea, I have worked here seven years and until I was recruited in to his so called elite ten without even a would you like to?" "He's been taking every surgery he could get his hands on and did not seem to be showing any exhaustion, we (his team) were the only ones showing that." We could not figure out if he was financially in trouble, which we felt was utterly impossible for his profession, however we all began to get curious. Was he on drugs? Big and dangerous questions to think about yet alone ask out loud. Most of the time we were in the Operating Room.

His surgical procedures required five nurses (At least that is how many he wanted in this Operating Room.) and the other five were either trying to sleep or trying to get a quick meal. I seemed to be the only one that never really got a four hour break. I have no idea why he almost always wanted me in the Operating Room with him. Outside the OR I got really good at sleeping standing up or trying to eat and sleep at the same time, however I know that is impossible, but that is how I felt. However, the short time we were together we devised a plan while we were all sitting there.

Chapter 10

Usually when Dr. Sampson would finish his surgery he would leave because he always had one of the other doctors close, by finishing the operation with suturing the patient up. We could not leave because we had to assist the doctor who was finishing up. By the time we were done Dr. Sampson had left the building.

Even though we all felt exhausted we planned for one of us, to follow him when he left. I knew it wouldn't be me because he seems to beep me all the time. We devised a plan. Sally volunteered to follow Dr. Sampson.

We all knew his car, so Sally was ready. When he walked out of the OR she watched and waited for him to change. Sally went down first to the garage and waited.

She had purposely parked the car near his but at a place where he could not see her. When she saw him enter the garage, she was already in her car waiting for him. She also knew he had scheduled another surgery within one hour, (he's going to be late, but what doctor isn't late?) She followed him for about 15 minutes and then he pulled up at a house on a street she never heard of, parked and went in. Sally made sure she wrote down the name of the street and house number.

He wasn't in there very long. She waited until he came out. He didn't seem to be carrying anything in his hands other than his black bag he went in with and he was dressed the same as he was when he went in, but still what the hell is in that house?

He got into his car and she starting following him until she realized they were headed for his house. He parked his car (he couldn't be seeing his wife because she left him along time ago) once again he wasn't in there very long, came out, same clothing, got in his car and away we went again.

All of sudden her pager went off. Shit he wants me to assist in his next surgery. I had to go a different direction so I could beat him back and be on the floor before he gets back up stairs. I made a few right and left turns and almost went through a red light, got to the garage, parked my car and went up the elevator. Just as the doors were closing he was pulling in the garage.

I ran down the hallway to the nurses room, changed clothes for surgery and ran in to start to scrub. Jane saw me running and wondered what was going on. I went into the scrub room to talk to her and just as I went to say something, Dr. Sampson came in and said Jane, "what are you in here for?" Her back was to him, she said "Well, I went looking for Sally because I wondered if she wanted something from the cafeteria and I couldn't find her so this was my last stop." "Well, I don't think she will need anything now." "Well, if everyone is ready to start?" said Dr. Sampson.

Jane was dying inside, she couldn't wait to find out what Sally saw or what he does. She went to the nursing lounge and Trudy said excitedly "Well, what's going on, what did you find out?"

"I don't know, she must of been paged on her way back'" "I think she just beat him back, which I am so thankful for." "I would not of wanted her to get caught, because he would of figured out we were talking about his unusual habits recently." "We're going to have to wait until we are all together again."

Chapter 11

The next day I had off was a Saturday when I had asked Sam if we could go out to Sundown's for dinner. I went home and tried to pick out a nice sexy outfit. This is the first time Sam and I would be going out in a long time. I want it to be perfect. I think I had about eights dresses on my bed before I decided upon one, which was the first one I had picked out, (go with you gut Jane, you think to much.) Sam was right on time, eight o'clock. "Hi Sam, how are you?" "Good, to be honest, I have been looking forward to this." "So have I"

We took a taxi to Sundown's and Marcelo set us at a wonderful window table. It was so nice to relax, enjoy the view with the man you loved. I just hope this lasts after I tell him if I have too. Sam ordered a bottle of wine and both of us relaxed and talked. We talked through every entire course.

"So how is your case doing?" Well, it's been very time consuming to say the least." "There was a hole in the last case and if I could have filled that hole in than I'm positive I could have won that case." "This is my second case in the last year that has tested my knowledge with the law." "I lost the last one, I better not loose this one." (Boy Sam, if you only knew, that I could fill in that hole of your last case.) I have to try and figure

31

a way to tell you without loosing you again. However I won't let you loose this case the second time, no matter what happens to us. I want him to win this case.

We had a wonderful time together. We talked and walked, trying in one night to catch up on everything since the last time we saw each other. We went back to my appartment and had a few drinks. Then he approached me as I was sitting on the couch and took me in his arms and kissed me so passionately that I felt like times before. I pushed him away, "Sam, I don't know if I can go through this all over again." "We had a wonderful relationship and then after that last trial you just checked out." "I know, that case really put a knot in my stomach." "I was so sure that we would win." "I felt so bad for the family." "I worked my ass off and I thought it was winnable." "I still think about it." "I only have six more months to try and think or find something on this case or I can't take it back to trial." "I do have some things that I have questions on that I didn't bring up at the last trial, but I don't know if this will lead me to breaking the case wide open or not. I have a few different questions that I want to ask the nurses that were in the operating room and depending on how they answer those questions will depend on whether I can break this case wide open."

Jane just sat there and took it all in. She wondered what he was thinking and what the questions were. Maybe I won't have to say anything after all.

"Have you talked to Frank lately?" "I know you haven't seen him for awhile. "Yes, we had lunch together." "It was good talking about the good old days." "He's great and busier than ever." "We are having lunch again soon."

"I really should not have left you two in such a way that I had to leave and not tell anyone where I went." "I never had a case upset me so much." "I never had a case take such emotions out of me." Frank gave me hell. "Well he should have." "You two are best friends and he even called me and asked me where you went." "Did he?" "Yes" "You have no idea how upset and angry he was." "You know he keeps an eye on you?" "He feels like he is you brother and bam all of a sudden you were gone." "I know, I will never do that again." "I hope so."

"We'll I think I better go." "I have court tomorrow with this new case and I better damn well win it, or I'm taking down my shingle and going to some island." "OK, will I see you again?" "Sure, but right now, I will be busy for a while." "I'll call you."

Chapter 12

The next day I went to work at my usual time, since I hadn't been called in for emergency surgery. Sally was waited with baiting breath. "Well what did you see?" "Your know it was really strange, he went to a house, which wasn't his, went in for about five to ten minutes, brought something out in his black bag." "Which I assumed was his and then the next thing I knew, I was being page for surgery." "That's when you found me." "I almost didn't make it back in time." "So who's house was it?" "Don't ask me, that's the fifty thousand dollar question." "We have to do some research right now, because if he is leaving town, I'll be damn if that is going to happen, I won't let it." "Also, if he is planning on retiring, that won't happened either, not on my watch." "I have walked around with this in my gut for over a year, time is running out, no one wants to talk and we seem to be the only ones that thinks things should be done right around here."

"Jane, don't say that." said Mary. "You and I have been talking about this for a long time." "I'm on your side, I said I would help even if it meant loosing my job". "Sally you and Trudy won't loose your job trust me" "It's the other two nurses that were in that room that might cause us trouble, but if we play our cards right, they won't even know what is going on." The next three weeks we just watched the doctor's moves and his travels back and forth to this house, which we knew nothing about.

Chapter 13

S am finally had some time to spare and we spent a wonderful weekend together undisturbed which usually very rarely happened. I usually never get a full weekend off. If I didn't have a date with Sam I probably would have been hot on the trail with Dr. Sampson.

Sam planned a wonderful weekend at a bed and breakfast place. It was a quaint inn that had a beautiful bedroom with french doors leading out onto a balcony. We drove into a small town up the coast where we had dinner and actually rented bicycles. The town reminded me of a place I would love to live in someday, but that sorta seemed impossible with are jobs. We went back to the inn and had a wonderful bottle of campaign. The next day we had a beautiful breakfast out on the terrace. It was a beautiful weekend that was so relaxing for both of us.. Of course, every time I thought about Dr. Sampson, I got sick in my stomach. Surprisingly enough Sam didn't mention work one time.

My wonderful weekend was over. I no sooner got back to the hospital when my pager went off. Gosh! I only get two weekends a month off which he finally changed if I am lucky and before I knew it I was back on the job. I knew we were going to be doing a lot of surgeries as usual with Dr Sampson. Before I knew it we were doing surgeries round the clock. He was back into his routine. I had not been able to talk to any of the girls. At least five of us were always in surgery some times six but that was rare, it had to be a serious operation. The other four to five girls were usually sleeping on cots or at least trying to get some sleep.

One day we were all in the nurses lounge. It seemed like a miracle. We finally got a chance to catch up with what was going on with each other. What we have been doing on our few days off during the month.

Mary made an announcement that she was pregnant. We were ecstatic. She had been trying for quite a few years. I said "Well Mary, it looks like you finally hit the right weekend off." We all laughed. Janet announced she was taking time off next year to do some traveling. She didn't quite know where she was going yet, just that she really needed a break and decided it was time to go away. After all she said "I think I have about a month coming to me." I thought to myself, golly I hope she doesn't leave before the shit hits the fan, because I will need her.

Sally and I didn't want to rock the boat yet, till we got more information on what in the hell he was doing, when he went to that house. I told Trudy we need more time and information.

Chapter 14

Sam was busy working on his next trial. He had told Jane he was really worried about this one. Facts were conflicting and he needed someone to speak up and tell the truth. That is my problem, who can talk about the problem with this trial when the patient was unable to testify. He had passed away. He had come in with difficulty breathing. chest pains and shortness of breath. When the emergency room attending physician Dr. Morris called for a consultation from cardiology, the ER physician suggested to Dr Dunmore that Mr. Conner, they felt could be having heart problems, His EKG was irregular.

Dr. Dunmore, the heart surgeon on call that evening stated after his examination, that he was having a problem with his lungs. He ordered the usual routine blood work, however never ordered a sonogram on his heart. He felt that he probably had some kind of pneumonia, due to the fact it was summer and this season was not a regular summer season. It was having his cold weeks and warm weeks. He felt that's what was effecting his lungs, or even stomach issues but not heart. He never examined him for any further heart issues.

Dr. Dunmore seemed irritated that someone had the nerve to diagnose a patient that wasn't trained in cardiology. "You know, you people irritate the hell out of me." "As soon as someone comes in with a little shortness of breath or chest pains, you always call me." "Why don't you get your act together down here?" "I have been up almost twenty-four hours and I don't need a simple pneumonia problem being turned into a possible emergency surgery."

"I am out of here, if you need me for a real emergency than call me, however I'm going home for some shut eye." "Do your job down here." Dr. Morris the attending emergency physician stood there with her mouth open. She could not believe what she had just witnessed and heard. She took out a blank piece of paper and sat down dated it and wrote exactly what happened and what Dr. Dunmore said with his unruly speech. Her notes stated his attitude and how he cared more about going home than caring about a patient. She finished the notes and folded it and put it in her pocket. Not long after Dr. Morris finished her personal notes, she entered into the logged following Dr. Dunmore's notes that the patient possibly had pneumonia per Dr. Dunmore and ordered an an xray of his lungs and antibiotic. About 30 minutes latter the gentleman went in to seizures and spitting up blood. Now they knew they had another problem. They called for an endocrinologist to do an examination. Dr. Rogers ordered an Upper GI and Dr. Morris had asked for a complete blood work plus type and cross. However before the blood worked came back the doctor proceeded to do the procedure after his seizures were under control. As the procedure continued the gentleman started loosing blood as fast as it could be administered. They rushed him into surgery and fifteen minutes later a surgeon Dr Samuals was called in to see if he could find what the issue was, why he was loosing so much blood in the stomach area. Thirty minutes later they pronounced him dead. However they really didn't have any reason as to why he died except for the fact he was loosing a lot of blood and probably had a sever ulcer but couldn't find one and they didn't get to it in enough time. Both doctors stated that they did everything right and filled out their chart as to what they did exactly on the patient that expired.

Chapter 15

Half way through the trial. Sam was in his office when Dr. Morris came in with her notes she had been holding on to. She asked to see Sam, regarding the case he was prosecuting on Mr. Emery. Dr. Morris introduced herself as the first one on the seen when Mr. Emery came in. Sam was unaware of Dr. Morris and her treatment of Mr. Emery. She explained what happened and what Dr. Dunmore had said. "I was a resident Sam, I needed a specialist direction?" "The chief emergency physician was tending to another emergency and I felt this was an emergency also." "We were short handed that night and I didn't want to take any chances, so with chest pains I called Dr. Donmore because his EKG Was irregular. ""He had SOB and stomach pains but at that time no other symptoms." "I was looking for some guidance but as you can see he didn't want to be bothered." "I took the information and asked her not to attend the trail. He did have a question about ordering a total work up on blood, done in the ER and what were the results? Dr Morris stated she wanted to do that but was over ruled by Dr Dunmore who stated he was having stomach issues and possible phenomena. Dr. Dunmore told her not to ever waist his time unless she knew what a heart attack was and under no circumstances order unnecessary orders on patients that was not necessary. So I didn't. I'm a resident and of course we are not up there with the high and mighty. But, I did think it was necessary just to be on the precautionary level. I guess I was wrong. The patient had been vomiting before he came in and there was some blood but, he hadn't done that since he was in the emergency room. When Dr. Dunmore blew up I called for an endocrinologist to scope him." "That is when I felt everything went wrong. "Why?" Sam said. "Because he died." The next day Sam went to court with a new theory about what happened and he recalled the endocrinologist. Your honor, I would like to recall Dr. Rogers. "Dr. Rogers please remember you are still under oath". "Dr, Rogers, when you were called in as a consulting physician, and expected to do the upper GI series, did you ever think there was something more seriously wrong with Mr. Emery?" "No sir. the symptoms he was having as described to me by Dr. Morris, appeared that he might have an ulcer."

"Did the procedure go as expected?" 'Yes, but as I started to do the endoscopy, I noticed that he had far more blood than he was expecting. Then his blood pressure started to fall and I called for a surgeon, that's when Dr. Simmons came in. I explained what I did and ""That will be all Dr. Rogers." "OK thank you, please be available for possible recall." "May the court call Dr. Simmons in please"

"Dr. Simmons do you swear to tell the truth and nothing but the truth?" "I do"

"Dr. Simmons, what happened when you opened Mr. Emery?"

"I saw nothing but a lot of blood. It looked like a bleeding ulcer but with the blood it was hard to see or even find where the blood was coming from." "I was just trying to stop the hemorrhaging "Had you checked his blood work?" "Uh, no I figured Dr. Rogers had checked everything and all blood work was normal except for his blood count down due to the bleeding."

"Dr. Simmons when you do this type of surgery, how many sutures do you normally use when you stitch up an ulcer?" "Six or Seven" "So sewing up a bleeder, by checking your records, you usually use seven to eight sutures to close an ulcer or bleeder, is that correct?" "Yes, it is. It depends on the doctor." "I have the autopsy report here in front of me, can you please read the highlighted area." Upon examination it appears that only four sutures were used to sew up the area in question in the stomach." "Could you explain why? Why didn't you use eight to ten sutures, which I believe could or would have stopped the bleeding."

"Well I tried to stitch him up as fast as possible, but the bleeding was so profusely that I realized he had stopped breathing and he had no pulse, I just stopped suturing him." "I made a decision not to continue because I figured he would have been brain dead."

"So you decided it was over for a 60 year old man and quit." Then he broke down, "Yes, that's what I did. I felt he was gone when I got there and I just went through the motions." "Did you ever find the problem?" "Yes, Dr. Roger nicked an artery during the endoscopy, that's why there was so much blood. "Thank you Dr. Simmons".

"May the court call Dr. Roger again." "Dr. Roger when you called Dr. Simmons for surgery did you tell him you though you nicked an artery?""No" "He found it himself." "Did you know you did that?" "Yes I did, I figured he could find and fix the problem before anything else happened." "Thank you Dr. Roger. "I rest my case."

Since the gentleman was only 60 and had a good ten years work ahead of him, plus Social Security, the jury awarded his wife $1.2 million. I was ecstatic!, I could not believe with Dr. Morris' notes and story would lead me in the right direction.

I couldn't believe I won. My hunch was right, My confidence was building. Thank God. I needed that win. I called Jane and as usual got her voice mail. I told her about the win and asked her if we could go out this weekend, if this was her weekend off.

Chapter 16

When my wonderful weekend was over with Sam, I no sooner went back to work when my pager went off. God, I finally get a 2 day weekend off and I can not even get my coat off and get coffee. Before I knew it we were doing surgeries what seamed like round the clock, rotating us in and out. I hadn't even been able to speak with the girls because they were in the OR with the king..... If we were off we were eating or sleeping. Mostly sleeping. Finally we were all able to get together. It seemed like a miracle but we didn't think about that long. Sally had followed Dr. Sampson again and right away we wanted to know what Sally found out.

Okay spill it. Well I followed him to a home at 2601 Tundon St. which was about two miles away from the hospital, which was not in a very good neighborhood. "Well what kind of house is that?" said Trudy. "I don't know? Then I followed him to another house." "He went in and was in there about five to ten minutes and left." I followed him back to the hospital, I must say I was pretty good, I beat him back in the hospital, just in time, what a miracle "Are you crazy?" they said. "Well, we have to find out what kind of houses they are." "One might have been a freak stop, because he didn't stop there the first time, but the other stop is not ""Either we follow him again or we go to the houses and try and look in the window and see if we can find out what is going on." "Sally do you remember where the second house was? "Yea, it's about one mile away from the first." "What we should do is one goes to the first house and another goes to the other." "We could do it when he has the other group of five in the OR." "One of use could watch him and if he finished before we were back, she could call us." "What do you all think?"

Chapter 17

A couple of weeks went by, when we finally only had five assistants in the OR. I asked one of the girls if I could borrow her car, because Dr. Sampson knew my car. I waited in my friends car until I saw him come down the steps. He started to leave and I started to follow him, until we came to that creepy house, Sally was describing to me. Once he got there, he again went in was there about five to ten minutes and left. I followed him to the next house and he did the same thing. This was the craziest thing I ever saw, this wasn't even the house he lived at.

Since he was returning back to the hospital, I wanted to get out and try and look in the windows, but as usual, my pager went off and I had to leave, in a hurry. I had to beat him back and change before he got back himself. Boy now I know how Sally felt.

After a few weeks, we were finally together again. He decided to take a weekend off himself. We went to my apartment. It felt good to relax, talk normal with out whispering. We were trying to figure out how the hell we could find out what was in those two houses.

Finally, Trudy said "Hey how about my boyfriend and I walk up to the house and knock on the door and see if anyone answers?" Our mouths dropped open. Jane said "That's a great idea." "Yea, No one would know who I am and I also could wear a wig and bring Dan with me." We knew that Dr. Sampson was flying down to the Bahamas so we didn't have to worry about him. "Don't worry about Dan, he is big enough to take care of himself."

Trudy called Dan and explained what we wanted to do and Dan said he couldn't wait, and wanted to know when they were going. Trudy explained they could go anytime, because he left on a weekend trip.

So that night Dan and Trudy went on there escapade to see what was going on. Trudy and Dan went up to the front door and knocked. A woman answered the door. "Yea, what do you want?" She looked like a woman that was very unattractive and didn't want to be standing at the door. They both said they must have had the wrong house. She slammed the door on their face and Dan said to Trudy, "I don't think he's in there getting a quickly, not with a face like that." Trudy started laughing.

So Dan said, "Well let's go to the other house and see what the next woman looks like." They did and ran into the same thing. Dan said "We were wondering if this was an apartment house and if there was any for rent." She started laughing so loud that I thought the neighborhood would here her. "I'm sorry, does this really look like one?"

"Sorry I just figured this was a building of apartments."
"Well it's not, it's just a big house. I'm sorry my name is Dan,
and we are new in the area, what is your name?" "Wilma" "Okay
Wilma nice meeting you and sorry to bother you. My dad use
to live near here and he had a doctor named Sampson, have
you ever heard of him?" "Yes, why? "He's my doctor, gee what
a small world." "He comes to check my heart." "He stops in
weekly to check me and give me samples." "I really can't afford
to go to his office." "He is such a nice Dr. to make house calls."
"I give him some packages that arrive here when he comes."
"He gives me time and samples for doing that since I have no
medical insurance."

(Did the elderly woman know what she was giving him.)
"He told me this helps him a lot because then he doesn't have
to go all they way to his house to pick up packages." "He says he
receives a lot of samples." "Oh I know what you mean, doctors
are pushed to the edge sometimes." "Glad you can help him."
Dan said.

She said "Please don't say anything, he's trying to get me in
for my procedure, because of my generosity of giving him his
samples." "Well I don't know him personally, my father was the
one that dealt with him." "My mom had surgery and he was her
doctor, so I don't think I will ever talk with him. "OK I'll see you
later. "Sorry to have bothered you and I hope you can get your
procedure soon." Trudy said

"This is really strange." "Lets go back to Jane's and tell her
what we saw."

Chapter 18

When they returned to Jane's apartment, they explained the entire afternoon they had. The girls were laughing so hard when Trudy was telling them about Dan's conversation with the second woman. However they now had more information than they thought they would ever have in just one visit.

"I still think there is more information out there." "What is in that first house?" When Jane thought he might have a possible drug issue, if that's what it was, that would explained his energy level and how he consistently is on the go, operation after operation.

Now drugs were an important part of the case, plus what I knew. Now he has two holes in the case. The two together could clinch it for him. But how do I do that? Just tell him, and have him hate me, when I love him so much. OR tell him why I had to keep quiet.

Well Jane it's time to sit down and tell Sam exactly what you know and also tell him why you didn't speak up during the last trial. I'm gonna have to call him or talk to him when we can get together and tell him what we found out. But once I tell him from the beginning will he get so mad that he won't even let me tell him the entire story.

Okay Jane how do you do or start this?

I decided to call Sam. "Hi Sam" "Are you free for dinner tonight?" Sure, it just so happens I am not scheduled for any meetings, and I am not scheduled for any surgery, at least until I get paged." How about if we go out tonight?" "Is your schedule free?" "It is for a change." How about you pick me up around seven o'clock tonight?" "I'll make the arrangements at Sundowns for seven thirty." "Alright it's settled, I'll see you around seven o'clock."

"Hey, what is the occasion?" "Oh I just thought I owed you a dinner for a change." "We don't get much time together and since I was off tonight I thought I would take a chance and call you." "Okay, sounds great see you later."

Jane got off the phone and started crying. Okay Jane how do you start this conversation? It's been building up from the day it happened and only got worse when Sam took the case. Which out of all the lawyers in Chicago he had to be the one to get it. Now he is so engrossed with the case, worse than the last one that swallowed him up for almost a year. Now this one he is working on harder and longer than the last one he lost. Well I guess I will find out tonight when I tell him what his reaction will be if I don't chicken out again.

Now what do I say or figure out when I'm going to do this at dinner so he doesn't loose his mind.

Guess what Sam I know what happened and I know you'll win your case this time. Guess what Sam, I'm the hidden piece of your puzzle or I can complete the case or you were saying there has to be a hole in this case. Well I'm the hole.

Guess what Sam I really do love you but couldn't tell you because of my job. I probably would of got fired. After one and a half years I just, oh shit, I don't even know how to start the conversation. Should it be at dinner where he can't create a scene or should I wait and invite him up to my apartment and tell him then. Or I could do something else entirely but nothing comes to mind at this time. Maybe I should wait a little longer.

Chapter 19

Since I just finished a case and was free for the day, I decide to call Frank and see if he wanted to have lunch. We hadn't gotten together for about three weeks. He said we could meet around twelve o'clock at our usual place, Harry's.

Sam walked in to the restaurant and saw Frank sitting at the bar. I went up to the bar and ordered a beer. "Hey it's about time" said Frank. "Yea, Yea, Yea, I can see you just started." Sam asked Frank if he was ready to go sit down at our table."

"Have you been busy Frank?" "It's been the same old stuff same as usual." "So tell me, you said you had won a case, tell me all about it I'm curious to see what's going on with you." "You haven't had a very good run lately so what happened?"

"Well, one of my clients husband passed away and I got his wife a settlement of $1.2 million dollars. That really made me feel good because I haven't been wining very many cases lately. It seems like I'm picking ones that I think should be winnable until we go to court and I end up losing, at which time, I was about ready to give up on malpractice or maybe even giving up on being a lawyer."

"Well, I'm glad that you finally won a big case and you've got your confidence back, because if something happens to me I want you to get me every dime I deserve?"

Sam started laughing, "Your such a bullhead, nothing could ever happen to you." "Frank, seriously how's business with you right now?" "It's pretty slow, my phone isn't ringing off the hook, nothing much is going on." "Why do you feel there's somebody you can throw in my direction?" Sam said "Not with the cases I'm trying now." "I really don't think I could ever through someone to you with the kind of business you do."

"But if it ever comes up I will give you a call, you know me."

"Hey Sam, how is that case coming along you told me about, that you've been working on for a year?" "Can't believe you're still working on that thing after a year in a half." "Didn't you loose?" I looked at Frank and said "Yes, I feel like I left my client down." "That Doctor should have been found guilty for malpractice and it just seems like something did not come out that should have during the trial." "I know. I'm right Frank." "Maybe winning this last case will bring me some luck in trying to figure out what happened on the other case." "That case should have had a very large settlement to it and I feel bad for his wife."

"Patience my boy patience that's about all the advice I can give you right now because, I know you're working your ass off trying to find the hole as you say." "You're right Frank but I know there is a hole that has got to be able to connect all the dots in this case."

"Well Sam as long as I have known you, you will figure it out, you care very much about your clients. "Hasn't the salutatory of limits run out on this case?" No Frank, if I can find new exculpatory evidence and it reverts back to the original malpractice or wasn't brought up in the first trial but goes directly back to the cause of death, I can reopen the case."

"How's Jane, you told me you were seeing her again?" "Oh she's great." "Frank, since we rekindled again after a year, it's been fantastic." "I think I am going to ask her to marry me." "Wow, that serious?" "Yea, she's the one for me."

"Oh and guess what?" "Kerry called me, he is going to sell his practice and has decided to move here." "You're kidding." "No, he said he got antsy and he just made up his mind one day to sell. "Boy, it will be great to have the three of us back together again."
"Yea, it sure will."

"So when do you think he will arrive?" "Soon, I hope, it all depends on how long it takes to sell his practice." "I talked to him about two weeks ago." "You know Frank, I'm gonna ask him to co-chair with me in this case I have been working on." "He is a hell of a closer."

Chapter 20

The group of five was able to get together again finally after about a month. they were trying to decide what to do. We were sitting there just relaxing all together and Jane said "That damn doctor can work our asses off and he doesn't even break a sweat or a yawn." Sally said "Who does he thinks we are?"

"Could anybody go to that one house and see if they can buy any drugs from that lady?" "Trudy, do you think that Dan could sit out front of the first house that you two went to and find out if there are any other people going in and out of that house?" Sally said. "Yeah. Danny has a week off from work, I'll check with him to see if he can stake out the house so to speak." We all started laughing, we sounded like we were a bunch of undercover detectives trying to plan a big stake out"

"But see if Dan can at least watch the house for two to three days to see if the doctor goes their every day or if any other people stopped at the house," "Sure I know he'll want to do that."

Dan sat on the house for a week. He didn't see many people coming or going in or out of the house. He stated that with so few people coming and going from the house it doesn't seem to appear that she is selling any drugs.

However Dan recorded as to how many times Dr. Sampson came and sometimes brought a younger man with him in his late twenties early thirties. Dan said that the younger man seemed to look like another physician.

We had no idea who this person could be with Dr. Sampson. The only other question that they wanted to know is if either doctor or at least Dr. Sampson carried any kind of bags out of the house. Dan said "He always goes in with a doctor's bag, so you wouldn't be able to tell."

One day Dan was watching the house he saw everyone leave. There was no on home. He called Trudy and asked if Dr. Sampson was operating right now? "Yes" she said. "Great, no one is home either so I'm going in." "Please be careful." Gosh he's really getting into this so called case. Maybe he will be changing careers soon.

Dan went in and everything seemed normal until he went to the basement. He could not believe what he saw. There were pills of every kind all over the place, bottles upon bottles of pills on shelves throughout the entire basement. Dan took a lot of pictures, as many as he could then he quickly left. He quickly got in a car and called Trudy. "Trudy, you would not believe what I found." "Piles and piles of pills." She said what kind?" Dan said "I don't know I took a lot of pictures I'll bring them into the hospital so that you can look at them." I do remember that some of them had names like Percocet, Oxycontin and hydrocodone."

"The others I don't know what they were." "Thanks Dan, I love you and I'm glad you didn't get caught."

Trudy was ecstatic she couldn't wait to tell Jane when we all could meet again. She didn't want to talk about anything outside of theses four walls. She would be afraid that it might get out and the story could cause irreparable damage.

Chapter 21

Sam was in his office going over his case separating everything into piles. He asked Phyliss to get everything he had on this case, all files were pulled. After he separated the files into piles he was looking at what he had and what he had to do yet. He sat down and made a list.

Number 1. Speak again with Mrs. Tunnel

Number 2. Talk to individuals who knew Mr. Tunnel to see if he showed any symptoms at work.

Number 3. Speak with the nurses that were in the OR during the operation. I still think this is the connection that I need to reopen my case. I spoke with the nurses before, but I felt like they were holding something back.

Well, I better get started, if I want to file this case away. Out of all the trials I have defended, this one seems to have gotten under my skin. I also want to call Mrs. Tunnel again, give her an update and to see if I can find out anymore information, that I already don't have. One little thing might send me in a different direction.

He picked up the phone. "Mrs. Tunnel, this is Sam, the attorney that defended your case against Dr. Sampson." I received your letter and I am reopening your case." "I want to tell you that I feel that there is more to your husband case and I am pursuing it," "I agree with you in your letter." "However I have to find something new to reconnect it to your husband's death then, I can reopen the case as long as it reverts back to the incident." "You see, I feel the nurses are hiding something." "Why would you think of that?" "Because if you had been there, when I question them during depositions, I just felt that I wasn't getting depth answers." "So, it's been a year now, and maybe they will tell me something they didn't mention before." "Well Sam, if you think it's worth trying, you know I'm all for it." "I agree with you and I believe they were not telling the entire story." "I thought I had asked everything I could, but something doesn't seem right or someone is not telling the truth, or maybe all of them, after all Dr. Sampson is Chief of Cardiac Surgery."

'However I don't care who he is, I would want to get everything told, no secrets." "For God's sake, they are nursing assistants and they took their own oath, I need to remind them of that." "I have been seeing one of the nurses that works with his team however she was not working that night." "I think maybe I could see if she can get something more from her friends the other nurses, if she opens up then I might be able to talk to all of the nurses or at lease most of them." "I will get back to you later when I have more information"

Chapter 22

After speaking with Mrs. Tunnel, I felt exhausted, just going through all my records again, I decided to get something to eat. I was starving. I pick up the phone and called Frank. I looked at the time, it was 1:30, I wonder if Frank had eaten yet, or if he might be busy with a case.

I picked up the phone and asked to speak with Frank. "Hey Frank, it's Sam." "Yea Sam" "Are you busy?" "No nothing, I can't push to the right of my desk" "Well how about lunch? "I know we just ate recently but I am starving for pizza." "OK I'll see you in about twenty minutes."

"Frank you know we go back a long way." "It's a miracle we still live in the same city." "Remember when we were kids and the stupid things we use to do, like build airplanes and expect them to fly?" We both started laughing. Frank said "Yea,"

Remember that time we stood on a board and went skiing?" "I remember when Kerry took a flip when he was on the board," "Now it's a big hit." "Boy we were stupid with not inventing that." "We could be millionaires. instead and sitting here having lunch and having to go back to work." We both laughed.

"I can remember when my wife kept forgetting to wet a washcloth when she had to change our baby." "So she got this

61

bright idea to use wet ones, which the adults used to wipe their hands, remember them?" "She said if it's good enough for hands why not baby bottoms." "Well me, not thinking about the future, we could of changed the ingredients a little and made them for babies and called them baby bottom wipes." "Boy that was a stupid mistake." "I have to give it to my wife, she was holding a gold mine and didn't know it. She had the answer but all she was happy about was having them there for changing diapers." "Well what's to be is to be." "Just keep working Frank" "Yea I know."

"Frank, do you remember when we were going to be pilots because we both wanted to fly?" "We decided to put our heads together and try and build an airplane that would fly?" Frank started laughing, "Yea it really looked good on paper until we built it and tried to fly." "Kerry looked so funny in that pilot seat."

"You know I still have those so called blue prints?" "You do?" "Yea, you know me, I keep everything." "No.... I guess that is why you became an attorney." "Boy, those were the good old days." "Yea, we were so involved in making things and going to the lake to swim that we forgot all about dating."

"Well, I'm making up for it now Frank." "Yea, you and Kerry should!" "I can not believe neither of you our married." "But I think I have finally found someone. She works at the hospital where I had that case against Dr. Sampson, her boss." "Don't tell me this is the case you are working on again?" "Yea" "I gotta make this case whole." "No one knows anything, at least for now." "I can't find anything in my notes that would have changed my case." "I have gone over everything again." "No one knows nothing." "That's where I think the problem lies." "I'm gonna start interviewing again, especially the nurses."

"Well, I think we should get back to work." "Yea, work, don't remind me."

Just then Frank's pager went off. "Well what do you know, they need me." "Stay in touch Sam"

We had a great lunch reminiscing about things that hadn't happened in a long time. Frank and Sam were best friends when they were growing up. Man we did some crazy things when we were young.

After a long lunch, I came back and got to work again. I'm glad I went to lunch with Frank, he gave me some ideas I might think about trying. I just have to talk to the nurses again, his famous group of ten. They never seem to be able to get together except Sundays, unless there is an emergency and Jane always seem to be called out on those.

Chapter 23

S am started reading his notes. Mrs. Tunnel stated that her husband felt pretty good when he returned home, however after about a month he seemed to have been getting his symptoms back again. She spoke to Dr. Sampson and he stated that he might be doing things to fast and to slow down, take it easy. She said he did just that. He took a leave from work and started gradually working himself up to full speed again when his symptoms became so bad that they called Dr. Sampson again.

Sam said I know by reading my notes, I covered all this however, I just need a few more details that might help me. Why didn't he want to see him? I was so wrapped up with this case and thought we really had a chance in winning I guess I wasn't through enough.

Did he follow instructions at home exactly as given. I covered that according to my notes. Did he want a treadmill test, how long was it going to be till his next check-up? I have that in my notes. How much medicine was he on? I covered that in my interview. It just doesn't make sense that he died. What did they miss? Or was I just on a wild goose chase because I won't except the fact we lost our malpractice case.

Chapter 24

Well finally, the girls got together and we were able to get together with Danny. We met at Mary's house, because Dr. Sampson knew where I lived and I didn't want a lot of cars parked around my home. Danny came in and sat down. "Now before I say anything, I want to show you some pictures I took an on my cell phone." "Oh my God, was about all I could say." There were piles of Vicoden, Hydrocodine, Oxycontin, and many more that didn't even look familiar. None of us could believe it. Why and where did all this medicine come from?

Jane said "Danny do you think you can play detective a little longer?" "Yea why?" "Well I would like you to stake out the other house and see if there is any activity there, except for Dr. Sampson." "See if you might be able to get into that house, if there is anything else we don't know about." "I just don't understand what this is all about." "It's not like him, at least not doing drugs or maybe even selling them." "He's got plenty of money. "It doesn't make any sense." "What is he doing with his life?" "It might take some time and you don't usually have the same weekend off to get together?" "I know, but we have to know what else is going on." "I'll start as soon as I can and let Trudy know," however he is in trouble already." "But, we have to be careful, we can't say anything yet." "This only adds fuel to the fire." Mary broke out the beers and we all felt we needed it.

"Dr Sampson walks around like he is untouchable." "However we have to collect as many facts as possible and then I will take everything to the right person." "I am really curious who is in that second house and who comes and goes."

Chapter 25

Danny was sitting in his car about 100 yards down, on the opposite side of the street, at the second house. Dr. Sampson does not know my car or who I am. I just didn't want him to see me. He never saw me at the hospital so I was never formally introduced, which was good.

The last two times this house had been watched was with Sally and Jane and they never parked, they just followed to see where he went, so this should be an interesting day and night. I hope she leaves the house so I can get in there and If I find more pills I'll shit. This man couldn't possibly have more. I wonder where he is getting them and from whom.

So here I was sitting, watching and playing PI again. We didn't know if he came here every time after surgery or just a couple of times a week. Maybe I won't see him.

Next week I am going to find out what it takes to be a Private Investigator. This is very interesting. All I think I need is a few things. Now WHAT do I think about next. Stake outs are boring. But someone has to do it. It's amazing what you think about when you are alone and just sitting and waiting. I'm going crazy. I have to shut my brain down. It would be nice to have

67

someone with you, at least you can have a two way conversation instead of a one way. One thing, if those girls send me out again, I'm bringing a thermos of coffee along.

Right as he was dreaming of his future, and starting his own business, good old Dr. Sampson pulled up, parked and went in the house. He didn't even knock, just walked right in. Boy, I wish I knew what was going on in there. I hope she leaves soon. She has to at least buy groceries.

Dr. Sampson came and stayed for about twenty minutes and then he came out using his cell phone, probably paging the nurses for surgery as to who should get ready for his procedure. How does that man do it. Well of course Danny, he's popping pills, and away he goes. But I really don't think he is. I think he just has a high metabolism, even at his age.

You know this house IS creepy. Now why would a man like him buy two houses that are not spanking brand new? That is if he bought them, and where did he meet up with these two women? Sounds sort of creepy when you put it that way and that older lady who said she was sick. Where did he find her? I wonder if she gave us the true story.

I can remember when Trudy told me about his house. Trudy was invited a few years ago, in fact they all were. It was a holiday party and she said his home was beautiful. Very large with five bedrooms, a large great room and quite a few stone fireplaces. The one in the great room was large enough to walk into and it went through to the kitchen. The kitchen had cabinets that were made of white birch with all glass fronts. She had an island in the middle with the latest and greatest electronic items installed. The only reason she knew about the inside of the house is because the wife told them to feel free to take a tour.

What a bragging sentence. They had three children, two were in college and one had just graduated college. Maybe that's why he needs his sideline job or what ever this is. None of them are married at least then, maybe now, who knows, who cares. I just want to get into that house across the street.

So now that I remember that conversation, this house is not the house they were talking about, now I know he doesn't live there. So, who is the woman he goes to see that he just waltzes in without a word, stays for awhile and then leaves. What is this nut doing? That old lady is certainly not telling the truth.

Next time I'm going to do research about PI classes and what is involved and what needs to be done, print them out so I at least have something to read. My I Phone is a little to small to use to read for something of this length. I'm bringing a tablet along also to write down my questions and also make notes as to times the Dr. or anyone else comes or goes. My brain is going a mile a minute. I have to see what kind of credentials I need. Okay, Danny, get back to what you are here for.

Chapter 26

I was able to talk to Jane one night. She called me and said she was home early and asked if I wanted to come over. As Jane was taking a shower, she was thinking how much she really loved Sam. Maybe sometime soon he will pop the question. After all it's not like we just met. We did date before.

On the way over, Sam was thinking the same thing, he had already picked up a ring, but as a man I was procrastinating about popping the question. It's even paid for. I've only been walking around with it in my pocket for 3 weeks now. I just got to find the right moment and tonight just might be the night. I'm taking the ring with me.

Jane was not only beautiful on the outside but even more on the inside. She had long blonde hair and a beautiful figure, however that is not why Sam fell in love with her, it was her personality and sensitivity. She was just what Sam was looking for, although he didn't realize that was what he had always wanted in a woman.

He hadn't realized it until he introduced himself to her on way to the hospital one day for an appointment. Out of all the women that Sam ever dated, Jane was the one that took his

70

heart. He thought that he would never find a woman to marry. He had his head buried in his books for so long that he figured he was bound to be single forever and than he met Jane and his life changed forever.

Sam decided that tonight was the night. He was going to wait till Jane had a weekend off but he didn't know when she would have the time so tonight he would ask her to marry him. Lets hope she says yes. I have been a real pain in the ass this last year but I think personally things are great. After tonight we can plan to go to dinner to celebrate as soon she has off on a weekend. Pretty soon I will be busy with work and I don't want to loose her again, like I almost did before.

That's another thing he loved about her, was her patience. She knew when I was working on important cases to let me alone, not bother him. I get so wrapped up in my work sometimes, everything around me gets put to the side. Jane never took that personally. She knew how I felt about my cases and the people I represented.

I knocked on the door and heard Jane say "Come in." "Hi, how did you know it wasn't a stranger?" "I didn't, however you are usually on time so I just assumed it was you." "Sit down, and quite worrying." "Would you like a glass of wine?" "No, I brought champagne." "What ever for?" "Well, please stop what you are doing and come over here, I want to talk to you." "But, I have to finish dinner before it gets ruined." "Jane, please, I need to talk to you." "Sam your scaring me." "Jane, we have been through so much this last year." "You have been so patient with me and sat back and let me do my thing and even didn't forget about me when I took off." "Sam are you leaving again, after this case." "No, if I do you're leaving with me," "What are you talking about." "Jane the day I met you I felt you were the one for me." "I never knew what I was looking for in a woman until we met." "It's not only the beauty you have on the outside but more important is the beauty you have inside that I fell in love with." "I have been waiting so long to ask you a question." "No I have been putting off wanting to ask you this question, because I didn't want to be disappointed and I was scared to death you would say no." "Jane will you be my wife?" I have carried this ring around in my pocket for three weeks now and first of all I'm tired of sitting on it all the time and I couldn't wait any longer to see what you would say." All of a sudden he pulled out a two carrot diamond ring. "I love you and I'm ready to be a couple for the rest of my life." "You are everything I have ever wanted in a woman." She didn't say a word. Oh God she's gonna say no. Silence..... "Jane did you hear what I said?" "Yes, yes I will marry you." "What took you so long?" "Sam I was not expecting this," "I was so shocked I lost my voice." "Okay now can we open the champagne?"

The next weekend Jane had off. Sam called to see if she was free so they could go to dinner and celebrate their engagement. "Yes, just so happens I am off this weekend." "Great I'll make reservations at Sundown's. I want to tell Marcelo the good news." "How about I pick you up at seven thirty?" "Sounds great, I'll see you then."

They got there exactly at seven-thirty and Marcelo set them at their favorite table. Marcelo said "So how was your week?"

"Well we wanted you to be the first to know." "We got engaged." "That's wonderful, I knew she was the one for you." "I am very happy for both of you, and the meal and wine is on the house." "Let this be my gift to you." "Thanks Marcelo."

After he left Jane asked Sam how his week was? "Great but very busy." "But then again every week or weekend is busy, especially when this case is coming up."

"I was wondering how Kerry was doing." "I hadn't heard from him for awhile, he also said he was awfully busy with work just like me, but he was trying to sell his business and making a move." "That sounds like Kerry from what you have told me about him." "He gets anxious, when he is to long in one place." "I wondered if he has finally found a girl yet." "I know there was one girl at college that he fell head over heals with but he only saw here once and she sorta disappeared." "We looked for her all over campus and never found her." "Gee that's to bad." "Yea he really liked her and only met her once.." "What happened to her?" "We don't know." "Out of all of us, Frank was the only one that is married." "I'll just have to wait a little longer and if I don't hear from him, I'll call him to tell him my good news."

Chapter 27

"Jane", "what?" "I went to the house, but no one came in or out last night except your buddy." "He's not my buddy, he's my boss!!" "Well anyway, I'm going to have to go out there during the day and see if anyone leaves during the morning or afternoon?" "I didn't get there till late afternoon and that's when the doc showed up." "I'll try and get there early enough before people wake up." "This time I'm taking a thermos and something to do." "It gets pretty boring just sitting there." "Besides I really like doing this."

"I'm thinking of making a profession out of this." "You do that Danny, frankly I figured you already had planned to do just that." "Well, I have now." "Sounds like we might of set you up in a new career." Jane started laughing. "You are really serious aren't you?" "Damn straight." "So if this happens what are we going to call you?" "I don't know, how about DANNY GET'S IT DONE." Trudy started laughing. "I don't know if that is such a good name, it sounds like an old comedy movie." "In fact that name would really have to grow on me, lets figure that out after you meet all the requirements." "Okay, but I am serious. I'm sure I will make a good Private Investigator" "Well lets hope we don't need you after this" Trudy said "Being a P.I. is a pretty serious job, and the most serious one he has come up with yet, and most original." "But, who knows he might really like it and by word of mouth in the beginning and he satisfies his customers, it could become a pretty good business."

"He can think fast on his feet and he did come up with some good ideas on this so called case we are working on." "So, let's see if he first proves himself."

Danny was back at it the next day, this time with a thermos of coffee, his tablet, printed information regrading Private Investigating School and a small snack. He was there much earlier and came prepared. He even brought his camera, just in case it was needed.

So now lets see who comes and goes during the day. Maybe this woman will go out like the other one and then he can maybe get a chance to go in. Danny started thinking about the conversation he had with Jane and Trudy about how they got their jobs.

"How long has Dr. Sampson been working Jane?" "Oh, I think about twenty years."

"Well you know my specialty, and one day he called ten OR nurses into his office." "We were all standing there looking at each other wondering what we did wrong." "Then Dr. Sampson came into his office and sat down at his desk." "He said that he has been watching all the nurses he has been working with and you ladies are the best of the best." "Here are your pagers." "You will carry them twenty fours hours a day seven days a week and when you are paged day or night you will be excepted to report to the OR." "You will be my nursing assistant team."

"That was two years ago and here we are still ten strong." "He still has built the reputation of this fine hospital and made it what it is today." "But maybe power went to his head now." "Well, Jane I'll let you know I'm going out again tomorrow." "Thanks Danny."

Chapter 28

Five hours later Danny was still at it, with no movement except for the doctor. He started writing times that Dr. Sampson would appear and how long he was there. However, he was the only one in and out. Never saw him carry any thing in except his little black bag, which I suspected was for show. After he left, I decided to try to get closer to the house. There was a garage connected to the house, Danny wanted to see if there was a car in there. To his surprise there was no car. Now how do you suppose who ever lives there gets out for groceries or anything else she needs.

Maybe the car is parked some where else or they left before I got here and I missed her but, he got here early this morning. He didn't want to get any closer to the house for fear of getting caught, however it still puzzled him, as to how someone comes and goes without a car. Now I have to watch the street and see if any cars park.

However, no one comes out. Maybe they leave from the back door. I guess that will be my next investigation. When he returned to the car and started settling in, he was thinking about his next move when someone walked up to the window and knocked on it. Danny wasn't expecting this and damn near jumped out of his skin.

I rolled down my window, ""Can I help you?" "No" he said, "I was going to ask you why your are parked here." "I saw your car has been here awhile and I was wondering what you were doing here, last night and today."

Danny said to himself, now what do I do? "Yes I was here last night." "The owner reported some strange sounds around the house." "I'm the police, Detective Tommy O'Reily." "She requested that someone watch her house last night and early this morning." "So that is why I am here."

"I wanted to see if anything is going on during the day."

"Well this neighbor has never had any personal problems." "Well she is alone and requested that we watch the house for 24 hours." "I understand she is an elderly lady and I can see why she is a little scared."

The gentleman started laughing so hard, I thought he was going to pee his pants. "OK" he said "But I think she is wrong, you can see we have a nice neighborhood and everyone looks out for each other." "This lady has cancer and in a lot of pain, so her nephew who is a doctor generally stops in daily to see if everything is alright and brings her pain medicine to keep her comfortable, and anything else she might need." "That's a shame, how lone has she been sick?" "Well, I think it's been about four months." A visiting nurse sometimes stops by to look in on her." "But it's usually Dr. Sampson."

"Well this is weird, why would she ask for someone to watch her house if her nephew stops by during the day." "Why wouldn't she say anything to him, instead of bothering the police." "We don't appreciate wasting our time on things like this if it isn't necessary, and it looks like it wasn't necessary." "I'm going to have to report this to my superiors and find out what exactly is going on with this person." "Is she alright up stairs?" "What?" "You know does she know what she is doing?" "As far as I know." "I don't see Dr. Sampson very ofter but when I did see him, he didn't act like there was anything wrong."

"We never were introduced." "My name is Harry Seltzer." "Well how do you do, my name is Tommy." "Nice to meet you Harry." "Well I better get going, I have to report back to my precinct." "I'm working on my own time and now it's time for me to go to work." Nice meeting you Tommy, thank you,"

As soon as I left I called Trudy. I told her that Dr. Sampson owns the house. "A lady lives there that is dying of cancer." What? Yea" "He is treating her and checks in on her almost daily." "Yea, probably giving her those pain pills." "I wonder if she really has cancer." "Remember Danny, that old woman that came to the door didn't look like she was on her last leg and had cancer." "Oh, you are right" "Supposedly he has a visiting nurse visit her during the week also, although I never saw a nurse come yet."

After they all settled down in the lounge, they proceeded to tell Jane about the second house. Danny told them about the conversation he had with a neighbor. Jane could not believe it.

So Danny found the secrets Dr. Sampson has." Well, we don't know what's in there but it doesn't really matter."

"This house couldn't possibly be legitimate." "He seems to be doing business with someone and I can't believe that one is really housing a lady with cancer." "But maybe she does." So Danny found out the secrets of Dr. Sampson head of the cardiology department and surgery. "Well we don't have to know what is in that one house, it doesn't matter." If we tell the police or if Sam does that's all we have to worry about and we won't have to bother with him any more.

Chapter 29

Jane walked into the lounge and said "Well ladies I have announcement to make." "Dr. Sampson told me yesterday he is planning on retiring next year." They all jumped up with excitement. They could not believe that after all these years that there would be no more 24 hour days and working weekends. "I think he might of gotten wind of that the case he was accused of botching up and that the attorney was working on gathering more information on it." "I don't know how he found out but so be it, Sam will get him before he tries to leave the state or country."

I had told Sam I would be free tonight unless I got paged. He already put the schedule up and I almost fainted that I was not on it. So I will be lucky enough to have a short evening with him unless he pages me, fingers crossed.

We ate at our favorite restaurant and sat at our favorite table. It was a corner table where we were secluded from most guests. Jane said "I just loved this place." "It was beautiful." "It's chandeliers, the beautiful fragrance of flowers throughout the restaurant." "Sam we are lucky to have found each other." Sam said "You know I thought I would never find someone." "The way my hours are and how I loose myself in my work, I didn't do much on the dating scene." "I didn't even go to the prom."

"But to be honest with you the day I walked across the street and introduced myself I knew you were the one."

"To my beautiful fiance, who makes me so proud." "Your everything I have ever wanted." Jane and "You are everything I dreamed of having Sam." "Right now we can't plan a date, because of my schedule and of course yours." "I'll have to talk to Dr. Sampson, so he can make provisions to give me time off." "It might be quite awhile. (or unless he is in jail or will be broke when Sam gets a hold of him, we shall see what the future brings.) "Oh I forgot to tell you Dr. Sampson said he is retiring next year." "Really?" "Well he's going to retire with a big bill if I have anything to do with it." "I figure you would say something like that."

The next day Jane went into start her rotation and was hoping Trudy and Mary were there. They were sitting at the table relaxing when Jane walked in and said "I had the best dinner ever." They stopped walking and both looked up as if she was half tipsy. She went over to them and sat down. Trudy looked at her and couldn't help but notice a sparkling object on her hand. She said "Oh my god, you got engaged." "Yes I did." "It's been about 2 weeks now, I had to get it sized and I just didn't want to tell you." They were ecstatic. All three were talking to each other at the same time. Jane stopped and watch them. She started laughing and they stopped and looked at her." "What" said Trudy, "This is finally an exciting day." "You forget we haven't had much excitement on this job."

"So who is going to be your bridesmaids?". Whoa wait a minute, I don't think I have even thought that far ahead. "We can't even name a date until I talk to Dr. Sampson" "Or maybe he won't even be here anymore."

"Wouldn't that be nice?" "Now Trudy lets not get ahead of ourselves." "We all will have to talk to Sam, after I tell him the story, there will be a trial and that could last for months." "So I don't think we are getting married any time soon." "I just hope he doesn't get to mad at me when I tell him the story."

"I am so sick of keeping this secret." It's been one and half years since the last trial. I know Sam has dug out the records, notes, interviews and depositions that he kept. He refused to throw anything out. I knew this case really bugged him. He kept saying there was a hole in this case and well, he was right, only I couldn't fill it in at the time of the last trial. was fearful of losing my job, but I am not anymore. Working with Dr. Sampson all this time has shown me that the money was not worth it. When we finally settled down with all the news from Danny and Jane, Trudy said "Danny is getting to be quite the story teller." She laughed. "Maybe this P.I. business is not such a bad idea."

Trudy stated she was going home for while. She didn't need to be back until five o'clock. When she got home Danny was on the computer and it looked like he was filling out a form. "Danny, what are you doing?" "I'm filling out my application to apply for P.I. school." "The courses teaches me everything I need to know to graduate as a certified P.I." "It says on line that it takes only six months to graduate." "I'm doing this Trudy." "I really liked what I was doing for you girls." "This will be a real start for me." "I could pass out my cards to attorneys all over the city." "If I do a good job at this, I will get a lot of business, just by word of mouth."

"I could get a lot of business and I can even charge what I want." "Of course, I won't charge a lot at first," "I have to prove myself to clients that I can do a good job and prove myself." "Then my name will be out there and clients will come to me."

"But don't you need an office?" "Yea, I was thinking about that, I think Sam has a small room in the back of his office, and that is all I need for now." "If he'll let me rent it out." "Maybe he can even throw something my way, like this case we are working on now." "Which he doesn't know about." "I really don't think he will need much convincing, considering what type of practice he is in, but you never know." "All that I know is I have to do a good job in my courses and pass with above average grades."

"Boy Danny, I have never seen you so excited about going to school and starting a new career." "I know. you know Trudy, I feel I have finally reached a plateau in my life that I feel I really have a good change of doing the right thing." "I mean, I finally feel I am going to make something of my self" "Well, I'm happy for you." "You know it will be slow at first Danny, but if you do good and your name gets mentioned a lot, you will get really busy." "You'll probably be working long hours as I am." "I just hope we find time for each other." Danny stood up and gave her a hug. "Trudy there is no one else but you." We will have time together, even if I have to come to the hospital to see you and lock us up in a closet." "Doesn't this sound better than my eight to five job when I couldn't leave work before." "Sometimes I'll be really busy on a long job and other days I won't be busy or not busy at all." "We might end up seeing each other more." "Well Danny, it sounds like you're on the right track for your future and I am proud of you." "But we seriously have to talk about that company name."

Chapter 30

Jane was sitting at the lounge table and she said to Mary, "Well, I have to make an appointment with Sam." "You mean you have to call to see him?" said Mary. "I know, I can't believe it either, but that's the only way I can see him because he's been so busy." "Also this has to do with a case he is working on." "He reopened this case again." "This one seems to be bigger than the other case he has ever had." "Besides I think he starts tomorrow with another case." Jane was right. He was in court as she told them.

"Dr. Cannon can you tell me what happened when Marie Dawson came into the Emergency room?" "Yes, she came in with a high fever and flu symptoms." "She was 18 and had just started college". "The symptoms she had were mild." "She didn't show anything more than the flu." "What did you do?" "I gave her an antibiotic to prevent any further infection, told her to go home and drink plenty floods." "You mean you didn't test her for meningitis." "No sir, the symptoms were not there." "The next thing I heard was her parents were bringing her in by ambulance." "She had lost consciousness, and her fever was higher." "What conclusion did you arrive at during this second evaluation." "That she had meningitis." "Why didn't you give her a test the first time when she first came in since she was a college student?" "I don't know sir, I just did not." "The flu has been going around and I just diagnosed it as a flu." "Do you always diagnosis flu when a young woman comes in with these symptoms?" "Yes, I do." The flu has the same symptoms as meningitis, but with college students they are more susceptible aren't they?" "Wouldn't that have given you a clue to the possibly that she might have something more serious?" "It seems to me that you would cover your ass by doing a simple test." "I object on the comments made by Mr. Hamilton, to my client." "Objection sustained." "Lets say that you decided that it was time for your shift to end and instead of doing more tests you wrote it off as the flu." "Your Honor, this is getting ridiculous, my client is a doctor and Mr. Hamilton does not have the right to speak as if he knew what the doctor was thinking." "He's not even giving him time to answer his questions." "Calm down, objection sustained." "You were just finishing a twenty hour shift, tired, frustrated than one more patient walked." "Am I correct Dr?" "Yes but that doesn't mean that is what I was thinking nor does it mean I was tired." "Forgive me doctor for putting words in your mouth." "You mean you wanted to treat her, but just asked the surface questions and treated her with having the flu." "No, I actually thought that is what she had." "Thank You Doctor."

I would like to call Dr. Kirkpatrick to the stand. "You came on at the three o'clock shift, am I correct?" "Yes sir." "So what made you decide that she was sicker than the flu?" "When she came in by ambulance one hour later but, from her chart she was seen about an hour earlier and diagnosed as having the flu." "What were her symptoms now?" "She was unconscious, her fever higher." "I asked her parents if she was complaining of any other symptoms?" "They said she had a stiff neck, achy and her fever spiked up further than it was when she came home."

We immediately did a test on her for meningitis and it came back positive." "We immediately put her in a sterile room, started giving her antibiotics that would start killing the bacteria immediately and also put her in a seduced comma." "We always put the patient in a seduced comma to make them as quite as possible so the medication can work faster." "Meningitis symptoms mimic the flu." "It causes inflammation of the membranes around the brain and spinal cord." "Stiffness of neck and back is one of the signs that mimic the flu symptoms, however one question should be asked if they recently had pneumonia or around someone with pneumonia." "Streptococcus pneumonia can cause bacterial meningitis." "If she was near that individual and came in contact with their fluids of any kind it can react to a point of meningitis."

"If you would of seen her first and treated her for flu, and then sent her back to the college, what could have happened?" "Well in my opinion she would of died." "It takes a very short time for this disease to go through the central nervous system." "The only good thing that came out of this is that Dr. Cannon sent her home instead of sending her back to college." "Now doctor, One more question." "What would you have done if you would have treated this young lady?" "Well, with the history of her age and attending college I would have done a test for meningitis." "It shows up in college students more than any other students in schools." "Every doctor should have this knowledge and act upon it." "Thank you Dr." "The plaintiff calls Mrs. Lee." "Mrs Lee, please tell us you occupation." "I am a physical therapist" "What was your job in this case." "After Maria was treated she had difficulty using her arms." "It was as if she was a baby again and had to learn all over how to do anything." "She couldn't hold anything." "We had to start with baby toys and work our way up to a child's grasp." "How is she doing now?" "Well after nine months of therapy I am happy to report she is almost back to normal." "I must admit that it took a long time with treatment and at first I was worried that she may not return to the level she is at now." "She still is coming in for Physical Therapy but her treatment is no where near the length that we were treating her in the beginning." "Have you ever treated a meningitis patient before?" "Yes" "How was the outcome in the other patient?" "That patient I'm sorry to say is in a wheel chair and not expected to walk again." "Thank you Mrs. Lee." You honor I rest my case. Now the waiting begins for the juries decision on Marie Dawson. I hate this waiting. This is where my nerves sometimes get the better of me. The parents and Marie wanted to stay at court, however I wanted or rather needed to get out and get something to eat.

Chapter 31

Trudy, Mary and Jane were still back in the lounge room, when Mary said, I can't believe that you have to make an appointment with your fiance. "Well believe it." "He's just as busy as me." "I just hope he wins." "What was it about?" "I would rather not say." "He talks about some cases that he is looking to take on, however he never discusses which one he tries." "It would be a breach of confidentially." "He also has been so wrapped up in the case I was lucky to spend an entire weekend with him." "All he does is eat and sleep on that case."

"He was so upset loosing that case, that is why he took a month off and disappeared." "He really needed to clear his head." "When this trial starts again if he doesn't win this time, I think he will disappear and I will never see him again." "He'll probably stop practicing all together." "He was so close to the wife of that patient." "He spent a lot of time with her." "He didn't say that but I can see it when he talks about the case." "Now we have this evidence on Dr. Sampson that I have to tell him about." "I don't know what he will say about this." "Lets get back to our case."

1. Dr. Sampson was working round the clock
2. He visits two houses, one of which is loaded with pills.

3. Dr. Sampson supposedly has a sick patient that has cancer and is treating her. We don't know why since he is a surgical cardiologist.
4. All of us think he might be taking the pills for someone or at the most addicted to pills.

This has to be a malpractice case. He is working under conditions of addiction which is a clear violation of a working physician yet a lone a surgical cardiologist." "He is putting his patients in danger."

"I really think that has already happened" "Well we got a lot of planning to do yet."

The next day I went into work and Trudy and Mary were running up to me. I thought they were going to plow me down. I said "What's going on?" "Did I miss something exciting?" "Is it good news?" They started laughing and said lets all go into the nursing lounge. "We don't want anyone to here us." "I wish you would tell me what happened?" "We will."

Chapter 32

S am was just finishing his drink at the restaurant when he received a phone call that the jury was back. He paid his bill and darted out the restaurant down to the court house. He met with Mrs. Dawson and her daughter and prepped them as to what could happen if the verdict came back in the Doctors favor. He said "I am almost sure they will come back with a verdict in our favor, however I just want you to be prepared if we loose."

You can never read a jury, when they are in court or when they enter court with the verdict. As Mrs. Dawson and her daughter entered the courtroom everyone was present and seemed to be watching them. Both Dr's were present. One in the court room and one sitting with his attorney.

As the judge entered, so did the jury. "All rise." "Court is in session. "Has the jury reached a verdict?" "We have your Honor." "Will the defend please rise." "We the jury find the defender guilty of malpractice." "We have decided punitive damages of $1.2 million." Also we would like to request that Dr. Conner's license be revoked for a period of not less than five years "Your request will be presented to the Medical Board, however, it will be up to them on the decision of what if anything will be done with his medical license." "There decision will be final." "The jury is excused."

Sam looked at Mrs. Dawson and she was sitting there hugging her daughter and crying. "We won Sam." She said "We won." "It's been a long time coming Mrs Dawson, but, it was worth the wait." Now Maria you must work twice as hard to get back to 100% so you can finish your college. "Yes Mr. Hamilton." "You'll be set financially that you don't have to worry about any bills, just promise me you'll finish college." "I will sir and again thank you."

"Now about the doctor, even if the medical board doesn't revoke his license he won't be practicing in this state." "I understand his medical privileges have been revoked." "If anything he'll have to go to another state and then he will have to pass the medical board." "Even if he does, this case will pop up due to his malpractice coverage going up in price." "Now Mrs. Dawson take your daughter home and you can finally relax." "I will get in touch with you when the settlement has been completed."

Chapter 33

The girls sat down and started to tell Mary that Dr. Sampson had practiced in another state, and all of sudden left in a hurry. "He resigned and came here." "When did that happen?" "Well it had to be about twenty five years ago." "I think he has been here for that long." "How did you girls find that out." "Well Danny found out."

"How did he find that out?" "Well, he wouldn't tell me" said Trudy. "What do you mean by that?" "I don't know how he found out." "But he did." "I think he has been dealing with drugs for a long time." "The heat must have been getting to close and he had to cut and run." "Well we'll just have to wait and see what happens when this information gets out."

Jane's phone started ringing, she said to them it's Sam. "Hello" "Jane, I won, 1.2 mil settlement." "That's fantastic Sam." "Are we going to celebrate?" "Well are you free this weekend?" "Hold on, let me check, I don't know if I have a free weekend coming up or not." "Yes, its my weekend off, perfect timing." "I can't believe this month went that fast and perfect timing." "In fact, I don't think I am even taking my pager with me, as far as I am concerned, he can page the second nurse in line."

"If he wants me this weekend, he'll just have to get someone else." I really need some time alone with Sam and I especially need it for myself. All these things going on with Dr. Sampson and what we have found out is just to much for me right now. I need to clear my mind and figure what my next move is."

"Oh Jane I forgot to tell you the king wants to see you." said Trudy. "What, why me?" "He better not be asking me to work this weekend because I'll tell him, I'm busy and I don't care what he says." "Well, I better go and see what Dr. Sampson wants with me." "I wondered why he wanted to see me personality."

As she knocked Dr Sampson said "Please come in Jane. (how did he know it was going to be me?) "Jane how nice to see you (what is he talking about, he sees me everyday except when I have my days off.) "Yes Dr Sampson, you wanted to see me?" "Yes, I wanted to ask you a question about one of your fellow workers." "Yes" "Trudy and you seem to be close as friends, am I correct?" "Yes Sir." "Does she have a boyfriend?" "Excuse me." "Is she dating someone?" (what is he getting at?) "Yes sir, she is dating someone she just met however, I have only met him once or twice." "I don't really remember his name because we didn't spend much time together." "My finance and I bumped into them at a restaurant, she introduced us, and then we went to our own table." "Trudy isn't much with dating anyone steady." "Do you remember his name?" "Yes, it was either Fred or Frank." I didn't pay much attention except he was a new one and she said she was dating someone new." (that's right Jane keep up the good story) "Does Danny ring a bell to you at all?" "Danny?" "No, not at all" "I'm sure it was Fred or Frank, that is all I know." "May I ask why you need to know this information?" "No, you can not."

"You know Dr. Sampson, it's hard for us to get together with our schedules, if we can get together at all sometimes." "Yes, I understand." "You see someone was talking about my team and that name came up." "Why sir?" "That's not important, that's something you don't have to worry about." "I will deal with that." "Gee, I don't know who Danny is sir." "I think Trudy said her friend that she is dating, works for a moving company and maybe that is why it came up, but his name isn't Danny. I think I would remember that name. only because my sister dated a Danny years ago." "She lives in LA." "Trudy did say her friend passes out business cards because he works for a moving company and tries to pull in business for his company."

"What does your fiancee' do for a living?" "He's an attorney, he works in corporate law, very boring if you ask me but he loves it." "Don't ask me when we are getting married because with his schedule and mine I don't know if we will ever get married are schedules are rough, well I have an idea and I can rearrange your schedule." "Thank you Dr. Sampson." "I will let you know,

His work keeps him pretty busy." "If you only knew how demanding corporations are sometime he goes out of town, and I don't know when he will be back." "I might not see him for a week or two at a time."

A quietness fell over the office, and Jane looked at him as if he was trying to absorber the big story. "Is that all sir?"

No, could you call the nurses in that were in the operating room the night Mr. Tunnel died?" "Sure." After the six nurses were together in his office he said."

"I want to review what you were told in the operating room and what I told you to say as to what happened during that surgery.." "Yes we understand Dr. Sampson, you don't have to remind us." "Jane let's not get sarcastic." "I'm not sir." "It's just none us of will ever forget what happened and none of us will ever forget what you warned us would happened." "Do you think for a minute we want to loose our job." "No, I didn't think you wanted to loose your jobs, however I just wanted to go over what I said again so it will be fresh in your minds.." Trudy said "Don't worry Dr. Sampson we have you covered." "Good that's what I wanted to here." "But I don't know why, they can't take you to court again." "They have no new facts that I would know of." "That's right." "Okay you girls are excused."

Jane said "Can you believe he had the nerve to call us in and say that to us?" "He must be a little scared." "How would he find out anything that's going on." Tracy said "I have no idea." "Well he will be terrified when I get off the stand," "Because I am going through with my decision."

Jane almost shit when she closed the door. "I can't believe he had the nerve to do that to us." "Well nothing is stopping me from telling the truth, and I don't think when I am done it will cost us our job.(Why would he ask about Danny?) I have to talk to Trudy, right away."

"Trudy, we have to talk but not here." "Are you scheduled for any surgery tonight?" "No, why?" "Ask Mary if we can go to her house so I can talk to you." "Get the keys." "This is really important." "Okay"

The next time she saw Trudy was at Mary's house. "She said what's up?" "Well what's up is Dr. Sampson asked if you had a boyfriend named Danny." "What?" "Yea, that's not all, he told me that a group was talking and his name came up, of course I don't believe that." "I think he was trying to get information out of me."

"Well, what did you say?" Jane started laughing, "Well you should of heard the bullshit story I gave him, although, he must of found out something to bring his name up." "I told him I only met your boyfriend once." "Briefly and I thought his name was Fred or Frank." "We only met one time in the same restaurant and you introduced us." "I told him that he worked for a moving company and maybe he was passing out cards."

"Oh my God, do you think he believed you? Do you thing he bought your story?" "I don't know, but how did Danny find out that he practiced in another state?" "He still won't tell me."

"I wonder if he found out about him visiting that other house and that neighbor told Dr. Sampson?" "Maybe, I don't know how, Danny gave a pretty good reason for why he happened to be looking at Dr. Sampson's house." "Know matter how much I bugged him he wouldn't give me even a clue as to how he found out about Dr. Sampson, but it seems pretty, strange." "Well you better warn him of what just transpired, then get this, he asked what kind of business my finance was in. "I told him, he was in corporate law, long hours and boring clients, but he loves it."

"I think Danny needs to park his car and switch to a rental if he is going to do anymore investigating, until this mess is over with." "Remember, he has to be dealing, he didn't get those prescription drugs just by writing prescriptions." "He might feel he is being followed." "Where did Danny get that information that all of a sudden his name is being uttered by Dr. Sampson?" "That's a good question."

Chapter 34

S am decided to bring another attorney in to help him with this case. He had a private firm and sometimes when he had a large case or a very important case he asks another lawyer to co-chair with him.

He has a good history with medical malpractice cases. Sam felt this case was to big of a gamble to loose it by himself and he hadn't heard from Kerry yet. There is so much information that I think Kerry can help me with. But I can't wait to much longer.

Kerry

Kerry was always a happy go lucky in his high school days. Nothing seemed to bother him. If he didn't get a high enough grade than he thought he should have, it rolled off his shoulders. Kerry was the type of boy that they said had a photographic memory. So cracking the books were really not part of his college days, needless to say, Kerry partied a lot. He made friends easily and for that reason, he was always invited to a Frat party or just a party off campus or he was with a bunch of guys at another house that students had rented.

That was one thing Kerry, Frank and Sam did before they went to college. They looked at houses around the small town in Happy Valley, found a great house close to campus and it was just big enough for what they needed, which wasn't much. One rule was that the house was off limits to parties during college terms. If they had a break in classes fall or spring that was different. Frank and Kerry called it Sam's law.

Now Kerry was also very handsome, however the difference between Sam and Kerry was he didn't have the gray hair and dated constantly. He had the gift to gab so much he would forget he asked two women out at the same time, which needless to say gave him a lot of aggravation which in turn cost him a lot of fun our last year. The word spread fast.

Kerry decided that after Penn State he wanted to leave the cold weather and go out west. He had a short stop in Cincinnati for about 3 months and walked out faster than he walked in. Why he stopped in that city he will never be able to figure out. He finally rested in Arizona. His practice started up fast and furious. He was good in court, he won a lot of cases that other attorneys would not touch. He was quick on his feet with spinning the case from the prosecutor winning to getting his client off. He was a great closer.

They had a great time in the little town of Happy Valley, a great college town. They all liked the atmosphere at the college, however they all wanted to go some place larger when it finally came to graduating. Kerry decided he wanted to go someplace warm and ended up in Scottsdale Arizona. He grew what started out as a small firm to a firm he could be proud of. Sam decided weather wasn't an issue and ended up in Chicago.

Chapter 35

Kerry's practice was getting so big that he could hardly keep up with his clients. Plus he wasn't the type to sit tight for long so when he realized that he might have to hire more partners he put an ad in the Attorney News, a newspaper that is nationwide for attorneys that are looking for a job or selling their businesses or attorneys looking to hire other attorneys. There was other news in Attorney News regarding articles on cases that made the news, but this paper was mainly for hiring, advertising for jobs or selling businesses. Hiring a new attorney was not Kerry's cup of tea, that was what made him leave Cincinnati so fast, to many lawyers. So crazy Kerry put his practice up for sale. It didn't take him long to sell the whole bundle, he packed up his personal items from work, law books, desk, etc and packed up his home and decided to go to Chicago. He wanted to look up Sam, but first he wanted to find a great location for his practice and after talking to Sam maybe later join Sam and practice together as partners. No one else just the two of them. He could not wait to see him. Kerry was never one to ponder on decisions. Three weeks later he shipped himself literally to Chicago.

He had lost touch with Frank and wondered if Sam knew where he landed, which he hoped was close to where Sam lived state wide anyway. It would be great for all three to get together if he was somewhere close. He had no idea what Frank decided to do but he would love to see him.

Boy I can't wait to see Sam. He had told me about some of his cases and some of them sounded like he could use my help. Not that he wasn't capable, however four eyes are better than two.

Kerry was a young attractive man with a personality that women liked. Blonde hair and blue eyes, the perfect dream machine. He had all the assets that a woman would want in a man, plus he was wealthy, however, he wanted a new challenge. He didn't know if it was a good idea and thought he might be crazy for leaving a warm area and returning to a cold climatic but he always liked a challenge. The time he spent in Arizona was a good time, however he was getting in a rut when it came to his clients and their subjects. They seemed to be the same old subjects over and over again. Cases were a dime a dozen there. However, they were not challenging enough. He figured that Chicago would be a city that would give him a challenge and plenty of variety. His clients were a variety of nature in Arizona but not as interesting as he felt Chicago would be and Kerry's strength was in Medical Malpractice, just like Sam.

One day he was in his office packing up things and Kerry gave Sam a phone call. "Sam how are you?" "Kerry Hi." "I wanted to let you know I'm on my way to Chicago." "That's really great, so what made you decide to move to Chicago?" "Well, I have enjoyed Scottsdale, and grew my practice to the point of it being self supporting, however, I decided that it was time for a change." "I needed a fresh start, a challenge." "I sold my practice for a great deal of money, and decided since you were in Chicago, that I should move there too, start up a new practice and maybe sometimes we could partner together." "You know me, I can only stay someplace for a short time." "Besides I think I reached my peak here, so I am on my way?"

"Well, give me a call when you reach your destination." "I do have a few cases I would love for you to co-chair with me." "Great I'll call you when I am settled in." "Where is the best place to park my office and myself."

"Greatest place is Michigan Avenue." "Great office space and apartments." "We are really growing here." "Okay all call you when I get settled in."

Chapter 36

When Kerry was great in court, he won a lot. He was quick on his feet with spinning the case from the prosecutor winning to getting his client off. He was a great closer. Sam was glad he was coming.

His practice was getting so big that he could hardly keep up with his client and tell. Plus Kerry wasn't the type to sit tight for long. So he made a decision to sell his practice and move to Chicago and start a new practice, or maybe join Sam's practice and be partners. Kerry never was one to ponder on decisions. Three weeks later his practice was sold and he packed up and shipped himself to Chicago. He had lost touch with Frank and wondered if Sam knew where he landed. If he stayed in Chicago or decided to go some other place. It would be great to see him. It would be great for us to get together, if he was somewhere close.

"Hi Sam." "Kerry, when did you get into town?" "Last week" "Can we get together tonight it will be great seeing you again?" "I also have some ideas I want to spin off you, to see what you think." "Hey do you know what happened to Frank and where he ended up, I sure would like to see him,"

"Well your in luck he works close to where I have my office." "Your kidding?" "Yeah, and believe it or not, he's been keeping tabs on you." "Well what do you know."

"Okay I'll see you tonight." "That's great, I'll see you around seven o'clock." "I'll call Frank and see if he is available, which I'm sure he will be." "He will be so glad to see you." "What a surprise it will be for him."

Chapter 37

Kerry settled in and It didn't take him long to set up shop and start his client and tell. Kerry was the type of attorney that everyone was drawn to. His personality seemed to match his looks. He seemed to be busier than ever and that's what he wanted. Although he wanted to be busy and wanted the challenge of building a new successful business, there was one thing he didn't have and that he wanted very much, a girlfriend, a possible future wife. He also needed an assistant. Between answering the phone himself and all the paper work building up he's drowning. I'll have to ask Sam when I see him next time

He started thinking about Serena, the beautiful woman he ran into at college. Boy, if she only know how many times she was on his mind. I just wish I could have found her and had the chance to take her out. I guess I will never know what could have happened because it never did.

The phone started ringing and startled Kerry, it was Sam. "Hi Kerry, its Sam, are you busy?" "No, not at the moment." "What do you need?" "Well, I have a case that I think you might be interested in and I think this one is right up your ally." "It would be a challenge for both of us." "Sorta like the old days in college when we presented cases together to the class." "That

107

does sound right up my alley." "Do you want me to come over?" "Yes, I want to tell you the whole story." "Okay, I'll see you in an hour." So, here I am, doing what I love, a case difficult to prove, a challenge and requires a lot of work. God, I love being an attorney.

"Hi Kerry, come on in and have a seat." "So Sam what's the story on this case.?" "Well I first want to tell you that I tried this case a year and a half ago." "You did." "What happened?" "Well lets say he had a good group of attorneys and it was just me." "I worked my ass off on this case and felt it was solid." "But his attorneys had a way of turning everything I was trying to prove, around and well, he won." "So why do you think you can win it this time and what do you think you have that is new, that can get this case reopened?" "Well, I found out that when his patient died on the table, he didn't go out and tell Mrs. Tunnel until about an hour after the operation was over," "That didn't come out in the first trial." "Mrs. Tunnel stated she saw the nurse assistants left the operating room shortly after Mr. Tunnel went into the operating room." "It seems pretty fishy that they left right away and he never showed his face to her until an hour later." "Yea but that doesn't tie him with a new mistake because he didn't show up to speak with Mrs. Tunnel." "I know but Kerry there is a big piece of information missing from this case that I know will connect him, directly with making a mistake in the OR." "This is where you come into the picture." "This is right up your alley."

"Sounds like a challenge and you know I like a challenge."

"This has to do with a Dr. Sampson and an operation that I feel went wrong." "For one thing he has nursing assistants that work with him in every operation and when I deposed them the last time, I feel they were covering up something." "Imagine, if something happened and they are afraid to speak for fear of loosing their jobs, or maybe he threatened them." "This is what I am banking on." "This time I want you to depose them, to see if they will open up to you and I want you to see his attorneys" "I have another case with them but I want you to surprise them with this." "You see, I am dating one of the girls that works in the group."

"Wow, so you think something happened in the operating room and they were threatened to secrecy." "Yes I do"

"Jane said he is a tyrant, and what he says goes." "Was Jane in the operating room also?" "No, she was not on the schedule that night." "Thank god, or it would have been harder to do the case last time." "However I think she knows something." "Unless the girls were told not to tell anyone, even within the group."

"His attorneys don't know about me opening up this case again." "I have got to find something soon, I only have six more months, and if I don't find the smoking gun soon, I'm dead in the water." "Now do I have anything substantial, no, do I think there is more to this case than what came out in court, yes." "This is why I need you to see his attorneys." "You are good at making people think you have something when we don't have much of anything." "Boy you really believe in this case, don't you." "I do." "Kerry, this woman is only thirty years old she has two children and her husband died at thirty-two." "Something went wrong in that operating room and I am hell bent on finding out what happened." "The hole is in the nurses stories." "I know it."

Kerry's first job was to go see Dr. Sampson's attorneys. Sam wanted to put a new pair of eyes on the case, it would be like starting a fresh case.

I do have to agree with Sam on one thing, I also think there is a hole and I also think it's with the nurses. They didn't tell him the truth. "I've got you a meeting." said Sam. He told him he had set it up with Dr, Sampson's group. Don't be surprised at the number of attorneys he has.

Chapter 38

As I walked into the building towards the elevator it seemed all to familiar. This place looked like the office building I walked into in Cincinnati. I had not told Sam that I made a quick stop there before I ended up in Arizona. I got the job but, I felt like I was in a class room. Everyone was sitting at a desk doing work for the senior attorneys, booking hours and trying to be the best of the best rookies so they got noticed. I lasted there 2 weeks. I walked into my bosses boss and told him I wasn't born to be an ass kisser. He stood up to say your fired but before he could do that I told him I quit and walked out.

Finally the elevator came and I got on. I plugged in the twelfth floor which is where all these big firms were/top floor. I looked at my watch again. I am just going to make it. As the elevator opened, and as he walked out he saw people scurrying back and forth with piles of case loads in there arms, a receptionist that looked discouraged that she couldn't keep up with the phone calls coming in. They probably had thirty secretaries working here also. As I approached the counter, the receptionist looked up and said "May I help you?" "Yes, I am here to see Mr. Locker." "I am Kerry Carson, I have an appointment at 9 o'clock." "Please have a seat and I will let him know you have arrived."

As I waited I looked around and wondered if I could ever work like this again. HELL NO. I like my own practice and helping Sam on big cases. These guys don't know what they are missing. It looked like so much pressure, which is why I walked away from Cincinnati.

"Mr. Kerry, Mr Kerry" all of a sudden I realized she was saying my name. "Yes," "My name is Janet, let me show you to our meeting room."

She asked me if I wanted anything to drink? "We have just about anything you want." "Personally I liked the old way water, coffee or tea." "Now a days they have everything." I knew where she was coming from. Very old school but seemed to know her job and had probably been here for at least twenty years. Speaking her piece is not something a younger person would do, if they had only been here a short time. "Well how about if I make it easy for you." "I'll just have a cup of black coffee." "Please have a seat and I'll bring it to you."

She walked out and shut the door. I stood there looking again at a long table which always looked like it could seat 25 people and usually it ended up with 5 attorneys at tops.

Soon after the receptionist brought me my drink, the partners followed. Each introduced themselves, one, two, three, four, five. I had gotten out my legal pad earlier, and as they introduced themselves I wrote their names down at the top of my tablet, so I could remember all of them. I always want my appointments to feel I am hear to do business and have done my homework.

How many attorneys does one doctor need? I could never figure that out. Holy Shit, no wonder Sam wanted me to co-chair, when the jury sees all of these attorneys and it would have been just Sam, he would of lost. These doctors always make sure they are covered every way possible.

However I almost dropped my pencil when she walked in. She sat down and could tell by my expression that I was shocked. She introduced herself as Serrena, their Private Investigator. I could not believe my eyes. It was Serrena. I had not seen here since college. The day we literally ran right into each other. I wondered what happened to her. I looked all over campus, but never ran into her again. She still looked the same. There she was and still looked as beautiful as what she did when we were in college. Her beautiful long red hair was an I catcher, as well as her beautiful complexion along with her personality. One beautiful woman wrapped up in one small package. I hadn't thought of her since my last year of college. I wanted to forget about it and had forgotten about her until I saw her come into the office. My life just got better. I didn't know she was in Chicago or I would have moved here sooner. Of all the women I dated on Campus, this was the one I fell for right away and in one day she disappeared on me. Now I found her again and believe me when I say, I will not let her go again. I think I'm in love!!!

I could tell from her expression that I had a look on my face, she saw before and I had to bring myself back to composure.

We met one afternoon in the park on a spring day in April. Actually, we really bumped into each other. I was walking and reading which is still a very bad habit of mine. I was not paying attention to where I was going and I ran right into her. I will still admit I am always walking and reading, that is a very bad habit I had picked up in college and it is still with me today. We just stood staring at each other for what seemed minutes. I said "I am sorry I made a mess." "Are you going to classes here?" "Yes, I just started and seem to be having a hard time finding my way around." said Serrenia. Kerry said, "Sometimes I loose all sense of direction." "Something my father said I always had a problem with elevators, put me in one and I forget which way to turn when I get off." "No that is alright I wasn't paying attention." said Serrenia "I'm sorry, let me introduced myself." "My name is Serrenia."

"Nice to meet, you Serrenia, my name is Kerry.""Nice to meet you Kerry."

As they stood there with hands together time seemed to stop. Suddenly they realized what had taken place and he let go "Maybe I can make it up to you, by buying you a cup of coffee, where is your next class?" "Over there I think, in the Brandon building" "I am taking up law." "What a coincidence, so am I, however this is my fourth year." She stood there and just stared. He was so handsome. His blonde hair was laying softly on his forehead, blowing slightly in the breeze.

His smile told everything about him. He seemed so at peace with himself and acted with confidence. What were the odds of running into someone like him my first day at college. They said their goodbyes and both went in opposite directions, but their thoughts were in the same direction. That was the last day I saw her. It was if she vanished into thin air.

Chapter 39

Good morning Mr. Carlson, I assume we are ready to conduct our meeting?" "Yes, I believe we are." "I did want to tell you that I am working with Sam on both of these cases." "Both?" "May I start out by saying Mr. Carlson, we do not have much to discuss." "Your client is very adamant that our client has committed malpractice and I personalty do not think he is going to win his case." "Well Mr. Locker, "Call me Chuck", "Oh it's gonna be like that is it?" "What do you mean by that?" "Well Chuck I feel we have a very good case and I plan to do my job to prove you differently." "You see, Mr Wilder feels the doctor you our representing is not telling you the truth and we plan to prove that in court." There were chuckles with in the group. "Well Mr. Carlson," "Please call me Kerry," (two can play this game) "Well Kerry, our client is willing to settle this today for $100,000 dollars. "We feel that is more than adequate." "This is just a simple means to get money from our client so he doesn't have to work anymore. "Mr. Wilder has no present injuries that eludes to the fact to what he has accused our client in doing." "You mean his up coming operation is not due to you client miss diagnosing him?" "No, I mean that anyone can develop a tumor of that size and this future operation can happen to anyone." "It just wasn't as large as you are reporting it was when he was being treated by my client." "Mr. Locker, "please call me Chuck", "OK CHUCK I have statements from doctors who state it is almost impossible to get a tumor of that kind at his age with out a doctor seeing it, also along with his symptoms." "It's one of the first things a specialists of his training would look for." "He didn't even call for any tests." "He presently has no real problems to speak of, Mr. Carlson." "Please call me Kerry." "Okay Kerry, he has no serious problems to speak of." "Are you kidding me?" "Your client has not been very honest with you Chuck." "If he would have discovered the tumor, and operated on Mr. Wilson when he noticed the tumor or if he noticed it at all, we would not be here." "Now as it stands, the tumor has grown, it has effected his vocal cords and he is only forty years old." "I have statements from the doctors who are prepared to operate on him and state that he probably may not be able to speak normally anymore and with the job that he has it requires him to teach seminars for his work." "That is something he will no longer do because of the tumor." "In his job, he needs his voice." "Well this is our final offer on the table, and my client feels this is enough to see him through his illness, pain and suffering he will have."

"You mean this enough to pay for his hospital bills and only that." "Mr. Wilder", "Chuck please," "Okay Chuck hows this; he has a family to take care of and the doctor doesn't even know if he will be able to talk again after the operation." "He has two kids that are still in elementary school with a wife that does not work." "What do you think he his going to do after that $100,000 dollar hospital bill is paid?" "I think you need to go back to your client and explain that this man will have difficulty getting a job if he can get one at all plus, his insurance will not pay the entire bill and his wife will have to go back to work which since she hasn't worked in eight years will just be like trying to get a job graduating from high school." "This settlement is no where near what we will be asking." "This family will need financial help until this man is of retirement age." "This man will only get half his income for disability and you know kids do grow up and need lots of things." "Besides they will have at least eight years of college to pay for." "So, I think you should take this information back to your client and come up with a much larger settlement."

"Well this is our offer on the table and my client feels this is enough to see him through his pain and suffering." "I guess this meeting is over." "You can take this offer back to your client and maybe he will disagree with you and take the offer." "You my sir are in for a battle." "Well, Mr. Carlson," "Please call me Kerry," "Well Kerry, I can assume this meeting is over." "I guess how they say in the movies, we'll see you in court." "I always wanted to say that." chuckling as he said it.

"Well sorry to disappoint you Chuck but this meeting is not over." "What are you talking about?" "Now, can we discuss our other case?" "What other case?" "We know of no other case that you had wanted to discuss with us." "And who is we." "Sam Hamilton and I are reopening the Tunnel Case." "That's impossible, that case I believe was settled in court." "Yes I know." "I feel you should call and have your secretary bring in the files regarding this case so you can refresh your memory." One of the attorneys called for the case file regarding Tunnel vs Sampson, he said it would be in the case closed section.

I sat there and gave then some time to review there marvelous work which is what they were thinking when they were reviewing it. "Well Kerry, we see nothing wrong with this case and how it was tried." "We tried this case in 2008 regarding a young man who died on the operating table with a massive coronary the doctor states he had." "We were not aware that you were coming to discuss this case." "This was a cut and dry case."

"This is impossible or we would of heard of this." "Well you you are hearing about it now." "We are reopening the case again." "We now have new exculpatory evidence that has been discovered and it goes back to the original time and date of the death of Mr. Tunnel and that connects this doctor directly with malpractice in the operating room." "We have the right to reopen this case." "This will turn this case 360 degrees our way and we plan on reopening the case." "We we'll be filing a motion to reopen the case with this new evidence next week."

"I guess you will just have to wait till we file our papers in court."

There is nothing new, you are just trying to open an old wound because Sam was so upset when he lost that case for poor Mrs. Tunnel." "This is ridiculous." said one of the lawyers. "Everything is in order with this trial and all information was reported." "Yes, you thought so." "I suggest you call Dr. Sampson in and readdress the entire trial and his story."

"This is preposterous, why haven't we heard of this earlier?" "We had to take a deposition and compile information." "So now you are hearing about it." "The information changes everything about this case, which we will prove in court." "We will file a motion to reopen the case with new evidence and send this information over to you when we have our case is ready." "It will prove beyond a reasonable doubt that this doctor is guilty of malpractice and the truth will finally come out."

Serrena just looked at me, in shock but with a little smile on her face that said she wasn't shocked. She knew how I operated and knew if I said there was something there, there was. However she didn't say a thing to any of the other attorneys. "Well you're as crazy as Sam." "If you say so." I got up slammed my legal pad shut and closed my briefcase. "Well as you said Chuck, see you in court."

When I was leaving the assistant told me to have a nice day. Then it came to me, you know she seems like the kind of assistant I'm looking for. I know she has the experienced plus speaking her mind. She doesn't hold back. I pulled her aside and asked her what her name was. She said "Janice." "Janice I would like to offer you a proposal." "What would you say about that?" "Well first of all what is the proposal Mr. Carlson?" "Well, I just moved here from Scottsdale which I had a practice I sold, and I just set up my new practice, but I don't have an assistant." "I'm totally buried in paper work yet alone trying to answer the phone." "You are just what I'm looking for, if you would be interested." "How long have you worked here?" "Twenty years." "Well, how would you like a change Janet?" "I'll increase you salary twenty thousand dollars if you would be interested." "I must tell you I can get very busy." "There would be no down time." "I mean we could work twelve to fourteen hours a day." "Sometime I partner with my best friend who I

119

am co-counseling with in this case." "Do you think you would be up to this challenge?"

"Well I don't know what to say." "I am getting sick of these new young lawyers coming in, thinking they know it all." "I must say you proposal is very interesting, and the pay increase is very tempting." "Do you think you would be interested?" said Kerry. "Your offer in my salary is very generous." "Well I think you would be worth it." "I saw you in action and I only need to see something once to know whether or not it would work." "You know, I'm going to gamble with you and take your offer."

"I don't need to look around here to know that I need a change in my life." "So who are you assistant to?" "Chuck" Kerry started laughing. "Well tell him he lost his assistant as well as his case." "So when do you want me to start.?" "As soon as you can, give yourself time to tell Chuck of your new position then give me a call when you are ready to start." "Here's my card." "It was great talking with you and I hope to see you soon," "Tell Chuck I said Thank You."

At the front desk, the receptionist said "Good-bye Mr. Carlson."

"Have a nice day." "Thank you and you have a nice day also." "I think your bosses are not going to be in a very good mood for awhile." "I just wanted to warn you." "Well it's about time, they always are on a high because they win so many cases." I did have a great day, I shocked the attorneys and also I know I hired an assistant away from this firm. What a day, I would love to see their faces when Janet tells them she is going to work for me.

I waited for the elevator once again it seemed like minutes, when my phone started ringing. It must be Sam. "Hi Sam, I just finished up with the meeting." "I think it went quite well." "Did it?" "Excuse me, who is this?" "Serrena" "Oh, how did you get this number?" "You left your business card." "Oh" "You think your pretty sneaky don't you?" "Sneaky is now my middle name." "How about lunch?" "No I'm beat, besides I have to talk to Sam yet." "Yea, about that meeting that went quite. well." "Very funny." "So Kerry if you can't make lunch how about dinner?" "I'll pick you up." "How do you." "Your business card." "See I am tired I need to lie down for awhile." "Great, how about I meet you out front around seven-thirty." "Okay I'll see you then."

"Yea, I do want to talk to you about that run in we had." "If I remember correctly we bumped into each other on Penn State College Campus." "I am curious what happened." "Well you'll find out tonight." "See you later."

Well here I was again still no elevator. Once again it seemed like minutes before one came.

I was walking down the street, it started to rain, great, just great, this is the end of my terrific day. I decided to take a taxi, since it was about three more blocks to my home. In Scottsdale it was always sunny, now I have to worry about rain, snow, sleet and good old sunshine. When I arrived I was exhausted. Mentally drained and wet. I took off my wet clothes and changed into something comfortable.

I plopped down on the bed and turned on the television. Flipped through the channels and finally deiced to leave the news on. Great the world is going to hell in a hand basket, they are trying to get democracy and here I am trying to get someone the same thing, only in a different way. Well I better call Sam so he knows how our meeting went and who was there.

"Sam are you in the office yet?" "Yep, I just walked in." "How was you meeting?" "Well they were surprised when I brought up the Sampson case." "They felt you were being a real pain because you were so upset because you didn't win the first case and you grasping for straws!" "I kept them hanging and told them we would be filing our motions and would send them over when everything is in order." "Yep that sounds like Chuck."

"Hey Sam, you will never guess who I ran into over at that law firm?" "Who" "Serrena" "You got to be kidding me?" "No, she is get this; a Private Investigator for the firm" "A PI" "Yep" "She said she liked investigating cases instead of studying law so she left law school and became a Private Investigator." "Well, I can't believe it." "Well Kerry, are you going to let her go this time?" "Hell NO" "We are having dinner tonight and I just want it to go on forever." "Are you going to see her again after tonight?" "Yes, but there is a problem." "What" "Well she is working on this case," "OH" "I will have to wait until this case is over, but I still am going to stay in touch with her occasionally during the trial". "Sam, she's as beautiful as I remember her on campus." "Sounds like you might be in love." "Yea I think I am." "Well that makes two of us."

Hey Frank has asked us to dinner this week, Cindy wanted to meet the nuts that he use to run around with. I don't think she believes him when he brings up our names. I met her once, she's a sweetie, I don't know how Frank ever won over anyone like her. She's beautiful and he has daughter that is just as beautiful. "He has a daughter?" "Your kidding, Frank a father." "Now that is something I never thought about, when it came to Frank." "I know, but she's a cutie." "How come he didn't say something at lunch when we got together." "I don't know, I guess the subject never came up." "We were so busy reminiscing about old times and you know Frank, he never was a bragger." "Well I can't wait to meet his wife and little girl," "He always seemed like the type to settle down first and start a family."

Chapter 40

I decided to lay down for a few minutes, when all of a sudden, I was startled by the phone ringing. At first I couldn't get my bearings, but then realized I was in my apartment. I picked up the phone and said "Hello." "Hi, it's Serrenia are you ready?" I looked at the clock, it was seven thirty. I jumped up and stated I fell asleep and asked if she could give me twenty minutes and I would be down. "Okay, I'm not going anywhere."

I started to freshen up and started thinking about the first time we met.

Now I can't believe that we are having dinner together. This is the answers to my prayers. He ran down stairs and practically jumped into her car. "Easy there Kerry, we aren't that late." "Sorry." "So where are you taking me?" "A special restaurant, which is a favorite of mine." "It's quaint small place and nice for having dinner." "It's called Sundowns." "No way," "What?" "That is Sam and Jane's favorite restaurant." "Did you ever eat there before?" "No not yet." "Good than this will be your first time and it will be with me."

After they got seated, Kerry ordered a bottle of his favorite wine. "Gee your wine is my favorite also." "Is it?" "Yes although sometimes I have a shot of whiskey when I am with a client."

"Your kidding." "No you meet a variety of characters when you're doing investigative work." "So I keep it short and simple." "I don't want to get into the wine scene when I'm on the job." "I don't want them to think anything, when I am questioning them." "I like tequila also." "Boy I wouldn't think you were like that." "I'm not, except I have learned over the years I do that sometimes." "It helps me get information, now don't get me wrong I don't have a few, I usually only have one." "You have to think about the individual you are with" A Private Investigator brain. "Sometimes you have to become who they are, to get questions answered." "You sorta have to have different drinks for different meetings." "It depends on who you are questioning." "Or who you are trying to get information out of." "I don't meet people for drinks, if that is what it is for, in a place like this and sometimes the meetings aren't in the greatest of neighbor hoods." "What kind of life do you lead." "An interesting life." "Believe it or not some men depending on the type, like woman who drink like that, they give out more information easier." "I don't know, it's like it puts us on the same playing field." "Do you really like your job." "I really do." "Like I said you would not believe the client until you meet." "I believe it now""Any shady characters?" "Well lets say some, but we won't get into that." "After all I have to protect my bosses and their clients."

"Now don't miss understand me, I'm not that type of person, I'm still the person you met at Penn State, I'm just telling you it's my job." "I wear many hats, at least with this firm." "Are you ever in danger?" "No never." "How long have you been working for this crazy firm?" "About 9 months." "I wasn't here for the first trial." "Enough about me, what have you been doing?"

"Well nothing as boring as your job." Serrenia stared laughing.

"When I finished school I moved to Scottsdale got the itch to move on and sold my practice and now I'm here." "What's here." "My two best friends." "Sam is the other attorney that I went to college with." "We are co-chairing this case." "Oh is that how you two got together.?" "Yea." "This case I must say sounds very interesting." "Do you really think you are going to win or were you sorta putting on a front in that meeting?" "No the more you know me the more your will know I don't put on fronts." "Well I hope we have the opportunity to do this again." "We will if I have anything to do with it."

After they left and before they got into the car, I gave her a passionate kiss, one that I had been waiting for, for six years. "We definitely have to do this again." She said "I agree."

We had a great first date. She talked more about herself and so did I. I must admit I was nervous. That was a first for Kerry Carlson. But this is the first time I found a woman I think I want to marry also. We parted with all expectations of seeing each other again, only after the trial, so there is no conflict of interest. I can't wait for this trial to be over. I think that is the first time I said that. Wait till I tell Sam about my date.

Chapter 41

"Hi Kerry" "Hi Jane, what can I do for you?" "Well it's difficult to talk about over the phone, I was wondering if I could come over to see you some day soon?" "Sure, how about tomorrow?" "That would be great, I am off in the morning, if that is okay?" "See you tomorrow."

Now what would Jane want to talk to me about? Maybe this is the piece of the story Sam said is missing. He said he felt it was with the nurses. So this is the piece of the puzzle that should give us a slam dunk in court. At least I hope so. But Jane wasn't in the operating room during that surgery or maybe she was and Sam didn't catch it. I don't know what else she would want to talk to me about. If I am right, she couldn't go to Sam, it would be to awkward and painful.

Jane got off the phone and started to cry. This has been building up for 15 months. At first I figured he could win without me on the first trail but that didn't happen." When Jane arrived Kerry invited her in to his office. "Jane come on in." "It's nice to see you again." "I'm glad Sam finally popped the question." "Yes he did, I couldn't believe it." "Well "Sam tells me you have someone in mind also." "Yes I finally do." "Did Sam tell you I literally ran right into her the first time I met her?" "I think for me it was literally love at first sight, however I than lost her." "Did he tell you that." "Yea, that was a strange story." "Yea tell me about it." Yea I wanted to ask her out again but never found her on campus." "Imagine the love of my life ends up in Chicago at a firm we have a case with." "What irony." "We had dinner together already and believe me I won't loose her this time." "Jane I dated a lot of women in my time." "Yes Sam said you really got around." "Yes I certainly did." "But this woman hit me so hard I just knew she was the one." "In that ten minute time, I just knew."

"So what can I do for you?" "Well I have a story to tell you. "It's actually is two stories." "One I just found out about." When Jane was done telling her stories she felt like a thousand bricks were lifted from her back. "Kerry you have no idea how I feel to finally get this off my chest." She was so afraid what Sam was going to say however, Kerry told her he would take care of what ever she was going to say and not to worry. "Kerry this is such a hard story to tell yet I know it was the right thing to do." That was what Jane had to keep telling herself. "I just hope I hear from Sam after you talk to him." "Gosh we just got engaged, this might be my one and only shortest engagement I'll ever have." Kerry started laughing. "Jane trust me Sam will still want to marry you after I talk to him." "Trust me." I'm meeting with him today so I will give you a call after we speak, but don't worry." "Yea, easy for you to say." Kerry started laughing again. "So tell me what brings you to me instead of Sam?" "Well there is something I knew and know about Sam's case and I couldn't go to him." "So since you are his best friend and working with him on this case I have to tell you and you can handle this the way you see fit."

"I really felt Sam would win this case without me, but he didn't so now I don't care what happens to me." "I have to tell my story." "This is my one and only time I will be able to get the truth out." "I don't know how you will handle this with Sam, but I refuse to let him loose this case a second time."

"I have two subjects I want to speak with you about." "One has something to do with the day Mr. Tunnel came into the operating room and one has to do with Dr. Sampson himself."

Jane, I'm going to call you and go over the first time Mr. Tunnel was in the operating room." "This will throw the defense off." "Don't worry though." "They are going to have a fit because I am questioning you about an operation that has nothing to do with this case, but just go with the flow and ignore Locker, because he will be having a fit." "Then after everyone is questioned I will be calling you as a rebuttal witness." "So don't panic about anything I say." "Okay if you say so." "I'll do anything to get this story out." "Great."

"Well Jane. I'll tell you what, with what you told me, I've been sitting here thinking and I don't think I'm going to tell Sam." "You mean you don't want him to know?" "No, don't worry I'll take care of everything." "Trust me he won't find out until the day of the trial." "Just remember to follow my line of questioning." he will be so happy, there will be no time for him to get mad at you." "Yea easy for you to say"

Hello" "Frank it's Kerry." "Yea Kerry, what's on your mind?" "Well I have an issue I want to speak with you about and I was wondering if I could come over to see you?" "Sure" 'I have to be in court this morning however I'm free this afternoon." "When do you want to come over?" "Well, I have to see Sam this morning but, if you are not busy can I come over this afternoon." "If nothing comes up which I don't plan on it I'll be free, give me a call before you head over." "Okay, see you later.

Chapter 42

Courtroom

K erry walked into Sam's office and sat down. "Well you ready brother?" "It's time to go to court." "Yea, I know, I'm nervous as hell." "Don't be, it will be fine." "I wish I had your cool attitude." "You have always had that." "Even when we were growing up." "Don't worry Sam, we got this." Kerry said "Listen, I've been thinking, you can have everybody else, but I want Sampson." "Be my guest." "I don't know what you will get out of him that I didn't but he's yours and I also want to question Jane." "Well that's fine, it would have been a little awkward for me to question her," "I don't even know why you are questioning her, she wasn't even in the second operation." "What's the reason?" "Don't worry about it." "There you go again." "OK she's all yours." "Great now lets go."

As Sam and Kerry entered the courtroom with Mrs. Tunnel, Dr Sampson was already sitting there, cool, calm, and collected.

ALL RISE

The court calls Mrs. Tunnel. "Now tell me Mrs. Tunnel what happened when Mr. Tunnel became sick." "Well it was about two months after his operation." "It was August twelfth, we were sitting on the back porch and he told me he was not feeling right." "So I told him we should go to the hospital." "I know he didn't want to go but I told him I would rather be safe than sorry." "I must admit he was quite reluctant about going back again, after all he had just gotten out about a month before." "He insisted that he wanted to wait for his Dr.'s appointment that afternoon." "What time was this?" "What time was his doctor's appointment." "Four o'clock" "By the time we go there, he was starting to have chest pains again." "His doctor called for an ambulance and we went right to the ER." "They rushed him into the emergency treating room, started him on IV's again and hooked him up to the EKG monitor." "I was so nervous I thought to myself, my god it's happening all over again I started to panic." "They called for his cardiology surgeon who operated on him before." "Who was his cardiac surgeon?" "Dr. Sampson." "He came right away." "Thank God he wasn't in surgery at the time." "I guess." "What do you mean I guess." "Well,........ my husband died and he was suppose to just do the same operation that he did three months earlier." "Objection your honor, that is the opinion of the victim." "Sustained, the jury will disregard the last comment.: "Go on please Mrs Tunnel." "Well he came right away." "He came out and told me it looked like he had another blocked artery and he would have to go in and do another bypass." "He said this sometimes happens and it would be the same procedure as before." "What I don't understand is why he didn't catch it before. "Your honor, please."

"Mrs. Tunnel, just keep to the question." "Okay. (Yes, I wondered that myself said Sam). "Proceed Mrs. Tunnel, what happened next."

"Well, they proceeded to prepare him for surgery and took him up to the Operating Room again." "I asked him why he didn't see this one before?" "What did he say Mrs. Tunnel?" "Nothing he just walked away and proceeded to go into surgery." "I saw his group of nurse assistants follow him in." "They are quite a group." "What do you mean Mrs Tunnel?" "Well they were nice to me the first time I was here." "Dr. Sampson is very lucky to have a good team, at least that is what I thought the last time." "Why do you say that, well after the second operation, I didn't see any of the nurses come out and talk to me like they did the first time." "What happened this time?"

"Well they just disappeared." "Why did you think that was unusual, was it because they came to talk with you the first time." "Because they came over and reassured me that he was fine, they would be watching him and not to worry." "He was a young and healthy man and would not have any trouble with some rehabilitation and he would recover with no problems." "Like I said before they were a great group of women." "What happened to you the second time?" "Well after the second operation, none of nurses came out and talk to me like they did the first time." "They just seem to disappear." "Why did you think that was unusual?" "Yes, because the first time they came out the second time they didn't." "In fact no one came out." "I saw the nurses disappear and I didn't even see the Dr at all." "You mean you saw the nurses leave but Dr. Sampson hadn't even come out of the OR yet?" "Yes that is correct." "I waited what seemed like hours except I didn't think it was." "You know what it is like when you are waiting for an answer about someone you love and how the operation went."

"What time did he take him into surgery? ""About five o'clock pm," And what time did you see his nurses leave the "Operating Room?" "About five thirty." "Don't you think that was very short?" "Yes I did." "Last time it was about five hours, of course he had more than one blocked artery." "Dr. Sampson said he had another blocked artery, however I didn't know if he had more than one or not but they weren't in there that long," "So when did you find out when Mr. Tunnel died" "It was about two hours later." "Two hours." "Who told you?" "One of the residents that was in the operating room with him." "You mean Dr. Sampson didn't even tell you?" "No sir." "Thank you Mrs. Tunnel, that will be all."

"The plaintiff would like to call first Ms. Cynthia Carson" "Ms. Carson could you tell the court how you became a part of this case?" "I work in the emergency room and I received a call from from the ambulance stating they were bringing in a patient with a possible blocked artery." "They said the patient needed emergency surgery and did we have an operating room open." "I said yes what is the name of the patient. They told me Mr. Tunnel. "Mr. Tunnel, that's one of Dr. Sampson's patients, isn't it?" "He just operated on him a few weeks ago he came through the emergency room then." "I told her I could get in touch with Dr. Sampson, that he was doing rounds but he did not have any surgery scheduled at that time." "I told them that I would page him. I talked to the doctor and told him that Mr. Tunnel. his patient was in the Emergency Room and that he appeared to be having sever chest pains and the ER doctor said he needed surgery." "He was sure he had another blocked artery." "He said he would call down there, however to make the operating room available."

"The OR called back down and told us to send him up." "I then personally followed him up to the operating room." "Do you usually do that?" "No but this man was very serious and I wanted to make sure he got to the operating room right away." "Thank you Ms. Carson."

"Are you ready Kerry?" "Yea, here we go" "Just go with the flow Sam." "I don't know what you can ask Jane that she would know, she wasn't in the operating room." "She wasn't in anything." "She wasn't included in the surgery." "Sam I have a plan." "Well you must have found something out or thought of something that will break this son of a bitch, because no one is breaking." Kerry look at him over there all smug, like he is going through this with no problem. "Don't worry." "Why do you think I'm asking Jane back as a rebuttal witness." "I didn't know you were calling her as a rebuttal witness." "Sam I got this." "Okay Kerry, your a closer, so lets close this."

"The court calls Jane Thompson." "Could you state your name and your occupation for the court." "My name is Jane Thompson." "I work at Greyson General Hospital in Chicago."

"What is your occupation Ms Thompson? "I am a "Cardin-surgical nursing assistant to Dr. Sampson at the hospital and also head surgical nurse in the operating room for him."

When you say head surgical nurse what does that mean?" It means most of the time I am in surgery with him." "How did the first operation go with Mr. Tunnel?" "Dr. Sampson performed a perfect operation and repaired Mr. Tunnel's blocked arteries." "Blocked arteries?" "Yes" "Your Honer I object to this line of questioning, I don't understand what the first operation has to do with this case." "Your Honor, I am trying to help the jury understand how we arrived here." "But your honor this nurse was not even in the operating room when Mr. Tunnel had his heart attack." "Over ruled Mr. Locker." "I'll give you some lead way for a while but Mr. Carlson, please get to your point, I'm curious where your going with this also" "Yes your Honor."

"Now Jane what usually happens when Dr. Sampson finishes his operations?" "He always goes directly out to the patients."

Frank

Frank fell somewhere in between Sam and Kerry. He liked to hang with Kerry, however he had to study like Sam. He didn't know what he wanted to do, except go to the same college with Sam and Kerry. His grades were above average but not like his two friends. It didn't bother them that he his grades weren't as perfect as theirs. That's why he felt such heartfelt friendship with them.

Frank was a great friend. They all liked each other, they were a great team, only Frank had the strawberry blond hair, so in that respect he was the odd man out.

How did three boys stay friends from high school through college and end up still be friends after entering the working world. They all liked each other, they were friends no matter what. In fact they acted more like brothers than friends no matter what happened. They supported each other in high school, stood by each other in college and kept in touch after they went their separate ways.

That is what Frank liked about Sam and Kerry, grades or wealth didn't matter to them. They were friends and that is all that mattered to them. But he knew that Kerry was always the one that got carried away sometimes and forget how long it had been since they spoke with each other.

Frank kept tabs on both of them. In high school Frank was not as popular as Sam or Kerry. He was just Frank. Sam didn't pay attention to his popularity, Kerry was free spirited and went with the flow and Frank was in between. Frank couldn't get over the fact that nothing bothered him. Out of the three of them, Frank cared what people said or acted towards other people and himself. He came from a normal middle class family and he had to work hard to keep up with Sam and Kerry as far as grades and popularity, although it didn't bother Frank if some people didn't think he belonged with his friends. His friends didn't care what people thought. They were friends to the end. No one nor anything would ever split them apart. They were true to each other.

The three of them met in little league baseball. They were assigned to the same team and soon after that they were inseparable. Frank enjoyed the different personalities they all had.

Sam cracked the books, Kerry the care free boy that everyone liked and didn't have to study hardly at all. He felt he was in between. Frank was the only one out of all of them that played sports. Sam cracked the books, Kerry was care free and crazy. Frank played sports. He played football and baseball although his heart was for baseball. That is where he met his friends and that is when he fell in love with baseball. So even though he kept his GPA up he ended up being offered a baseball scholarship to Penn State.

However since Kerry and Sam knew what they were going to be attorneys, Frank didn't, so when Frank went to Penn State he went in as undecided. He knew his grades were high enough however his interest was not becoming a lawyer, that was about it. He figured he would find his way after graduation and see what might grab his interest.

Sam and Kerry never put pressure on him as to what he wanted. They didn't care, they were just glad they were all together.

After college he decided to go to Chicago with Sam. He liked the big city scene and since Sam, one of his best friends felt the same way, they went together. Sam settled into his private practice and Frank went from idea to idea. He finally found his place in society and settled down into the life he was going to love as years went by.

Kerry had to speak with Frank, it was vitally important that he get to him as soon as possible, There court date was approaching quickly and the information that he had, had to be told to Frank if they wanted this case to come together. I guess Frank is going to be part of this case even if he never wanted to be. He was hoping he was giving Frank enough time to do some research for him as soon as possible. I think Frank will be happy for the change of his routine cases.

Chapter 43

Courtroom

"Have you always worked with Dr. Sampson?" "Yes, when I started doing cardiac-surgery I was there for closing doing numerous operations with Dr. Sampson and he asked me one day if I would like to assist him from now on along with nine other nurses." "How does your schedule work?" Well we are required to work and be available twenty four hours a day seven days a week" "We usually rotate between operations." "He finishes one and when within an hour he starts another." "This requires us to usually stay at the hospital all the time." "All the time?" "Don't you get any time off at all?" "Your Honor what does this have to do with the case?" "Your Honor, I'm trying to familiarize myself with the working back ground of his team." "Overruled." "You may continue Ms. Thompson." "When the operating section of the hospital was redesigned we finally had a lounge/sleeping section. It was designed for us, so sometimes if we work round the clock we had somewhere to lay our head or eat." The judge said "I would like to ask a question?" "Certainly your Honor." (Kerry said be my guest, this sounds very interesting how he has this set up). "Do you ever get time off?" "Yes every month we get a weekend and then sometimes we get a day off during the week." "Continue Mr. Carlson" "Certainly your Honor."

"Now how long has this been going on?" "I would say about a year in a half." "Don't you get tired." "Yes, I'm pretty good at sleeping standing up." "How does the doctor get in touch with you if you are not in the area?" "We always get paged even if we are In the lounge." "How did you get your pagers?" "He handed them to us when he created the team and said carry these twenty-four seven." "We are basicly glued to them now." "He said when you are paged you will be expected to report to the operating room." "Couldn't you refuse?" "Who would refuse the Head of Cardiac Surgery?" "Your Honor she is giving a one sided opinion that question should be kept for Dr. Sampson to answer." "Sustained." "Now what was the group of ten called?" "Nursing Assistants." "We would be known as his nursing assistant team." "I told him I would." "How long have you been doing this?" "Oh I would say about one and a half years." "Have you assisted him with every surgery?" "Yes I have, well every time I was scheduled for surgery." "How many times does the doctor do surgery?" "He operates every day of the week and sometimes weekends, unless like this time when there is an emergency." "Does he usually always do emergencies?" "Yes however there are other qualified cardiac surgeons, but yes he does all emergencies unless he is not in the hospital at the time the team receives the call." "If he is close enough I will tell them that Dr. Sampson was available to do the surgery and he would come in and do it. How many other medical team individuals were in the operating room." "There is one cardiac resident, five nursing assistants, and an anesthesiologist." "Why did he have five nursing assistants?" "That I don't know the answer to you will have to ask Dr.

Sampson." "Now, how long did the procedure take?" "I logged him in at twelve thirty and at four thirty he was finished and done with the operation". "You mean he walked out?" "Yes, he told one of the other cardiac physicians to close and he left." "Were you there for the completion of the surgery." "Yes." "Did anyone else leave?" "No." "So you are saying everyone was there except Dr. Sampson during the first operation." "Yes." "Now, did Dr. Sampson follow up with his patient in postoperative care?" "I object your honor, how is this relevant to her line of questioning?" "I just wanted to get an idea as to how and what happens after Dr. Sampson is done with surgery, since I wasn't here for the first trial." "Your Honor" "Well Mr. Carlson, you can ask Dr. Sampson that question and we don't need your unnecessary comments." "Sustained" "How many emergency surgeries have you assisted with Dr. Sampson." "I really can't answer that question, because of the time I have worked with him." "I can only answer by saying many." "Oh right that is a fair answer."

"Please tell me, how did the surgery go the first time?" "It was uneventful." "What do you mean by that it was uneventful?" "There was not any problems with the first operation." "You mean you had no problems with the first operation?" "Your Honor what kind of question is that, he already asked it once." "Sustained" "Was there any other physicians in the operating room with you?" "Yes Dr. Thomas and a surgical resident." "When Dr. Sampson was finished with the surgery, did he close, meaning did he entirely complete the procedure?" "No Dr. Thomas took over when Dr. Sampson was finished."

"What did he do?" Your Honor he keeps asking the same questions over and over." "Yes you are Mr. Carlson, please wrap it up."

"Your Honor what is the purpose of questioning this individual when she was not in the operating room at the time of the incident." "Well your Honor I just wanted to question one of nurses that had a lot of logged in hours with Dr. Sampson in the operating room since I wasn't here for the first trial." "Over ruled, however Mr. Carlson, please wrap it up." "Yes, your Honor."

"Alright, when the operation was complete did you follow the patient to recovery?" "Yes, I did." "I was with him the entire time he was in recovery." "I do this with all of Dr. Sampson's patients." "He was in recovery about an hour until he was semi conscience, I called Dr. Sampson and told him his vitals were normal, his EKG was good and asked him if I could send him to intensive care." "He told me it was alright but have intensive care call him when he was settled."

"Did you see Mr. Tunnel after that?" "No after they go to intensive care my job is done." "Did Dr. Sampson have any more surgey's that day?" ""Yes he had one scheduled an hour later." "Have you ever seen Dr. Sampson get tired during any one of these operations." "No."

"One more question Ms. Thompson." "How many hours do you work?" "Your Honor, this is getting ridiculous." "MR. Carlson, wrap it up." "Yes your Honor." "Overruled, you may answer the question." "Well I don't know because we rotate in and out of surgery. Unless there is an emergency surgery." "I mean we could also be called into emergency surgery if there is one and we are not scheduled." "So Dr. Sampson works almost round the clock?" "Your Honor I object, she doesn't know how many hours Dr. Sampson works, she isn't tied to his hip." "I agree" "Sustained."

"Thank you Ms. Thompson." "That will be all for now however, please make yourself available if needed for recall."

Mr. Locker turned to Dr. Sampson and said "Why would he want her available for recall?" "Is there anything I should know?" Dr. Sampson said "No I don't understand."

Chapter 44

"May the plaintiff call Dr. Sampson please." "Good morning Dr. Sampson my name is Kerry Carlson" "Sir, please state your name for the court." "Dr. Charles Sampson." "And your title?" "I'm chief cardiologist of the cardiology department""Alright Dr. Sampson now that I have an idea of how your schedules work." "Lets get to the second surgery." "Please tell me what happened." "Well about 5:00 I was paged that Trudy I mean Ms. Smith was on the phone." "She said that a patient was coming in that I previously did surgery on about three months ago." "His name was Mr. Sampson and she was reserving an Operating Room.""Is Ms. Smith one of the nursing assistants on your team." "Yes." "Did she assist in this second surgery?" "Yes"

"When did Mr. Sampson arrive?" "I think about twenty minutes after five." "His Dr's office is not far from the hospital." "She told me he was coming by ambulance I told her to alert the emergency room that he was coming and to let me know when he arrived."

"About twenty minutes later I got the call from Ms. Smith." "I asked that he be brought up to the operating floor and that I would meet them there." "I was already getting a team assembled for the surgery."

"Do you always do that?" "Yes usually I have a team ready, however when it is this sudden I usually have to page them because it's unscheduled." "Some are usually there because they are working and some might have to come in." "Each nurse wears pagers and when they are paged they report to the operating room." "You mean you do not have a specific team set up for emergency surgeries?" "No" I have specific nurses for specific emergency surgeries." "Usually I page every one for an emergency surgery because I don't know who is working and who isn't." "How many do you have for emergency surgeries?" "I always have a team of five." "I also have a list of doctors that works with me in the hospital and I check to see who is available." "So you set the team." "Yes I do."." "Had you worked with this so called team before?" "Yes I have" "Maybe not the same ones together, but yes I have worked with them all."

"Now tell me what happened next." "Well, before they brought Mr. Tunnel up and they brought him into the operating room, one of the nurses drew blood for cross and type." "Why did you do this again when he was just there three months ago?" "We always do that." "It's routine." "When he was ready I was called and said he was in the operating room ready for surgery." "I went in and told my staff that Mr. Sampson possibly had another blocked artery and we had to do another procedure on him."

"Could you please tell us what the procedure is for a blocked artery?"

"Yes, it's when you restore blood to the heart." "It involves sewing a vein or artery in place at the sight beyond the blocked or narrowed coronary artery to restore the blood flow to the heart."

"Now on the day of March 9, 2007 please tell me in your words exactly what happened in the operating room that day."

"Well when the anesthesiologist told me he was ready for surgery, I started the procedure, however all of a sudden his vitals dropped." "He started to go into cardiac arrest." "We tried everything, we used a defibrillator on him and gave him an anti-arrhythmic drug." "There was no response." "How long did you work on Mr. Sampson?" "About thirty minutes." "At 6:10 we pronounced him dead."

"What happened next?" "I asked Dr. Douglas to close and I left the operating room." "So how long were you in the operating room?" "I'd say about forty five minutes." "Thank you Dr. Sampson."

Mr. Locker said "Just a minute Dr. Sampson, I have a few questions for you." "When you were finished why didn't you go out to Mrs. Sampson right away." "Well, I had paper work to fill out." "We do this right after we loose a patient so I can write down all the details while they are fresh in my mind." "Is this the same procedure you do for every death you have?" "Yes it is." "How long after Mr. Sampson passed away did you go out to see Mrs. Sampson?" "It was about an hour after I came out of the operating room."

"Thank you Dr. Sampson."

I have another question Dr. Sampson." said Kerry. "How long does it take for a patient to heal from this procedure?" "It takes about five to six months for the patient to start to really get back to normal, in respect to his health." "How about his operation in general." "What do you mean?" "I mean how about his incisions?" "Well the main incision takes about four months to heal to the point of not being soft or tender and create scar tissue." "It takes quite awhile for your ribs to heal."

"Thank you Dr. Sampson."

Chapter 45

"The plaintiff calls Ms. Tracy Smith." "Ms. Smith could you state you name please for the court." "Yes Ms. Tracy Smith". "Ms. Smith could you please tell us what you observed in the operating room." "Well as Dr. Sampson stated we were about to start the procedure when Mr. Tunnel went into cardiac arrest." "We tried everything we could to save him however it was just to late." "Thank you that will be all." "However please make yourself available for recall if needed."

"I have a few questions Ms. Smith." "Did Dr. Sampson do anything different when he was working on Mr. Tunnel?" "No" "Thank you."

As each nursing assistant continued to be called up to the testify, they all seemed to say the exact thing and Dr. Sampson's attorney asked the exact same question.

Sam leaned over to Kerry and said "Did you pick up on all the nursing assistants stating the exact same thing, word for word." "Yea I did." "Interesting." "You know last time their answers were not word for word. "That's what I find very interesting." "See I told you there was a hole in the nurses testimony." "Yea, well just wait till I speak with Jane again."

"Why do you have to talk with Jane again?" "You'll see." "I have it figured out."

Sam said "It seemed like maybe someone had a meeting before court today." "It sounds like it." "I think he thinks he is in the clear." "I got this." "What do you have?" "Don't worry I got this Sam." "Okay it's now in your hands." "You know something I don't know?" "Yes I do, just watch."

Chapter 46

"I would like to recall Ms. Jane Thompson please." "Ms. Thompson I would like to remind you, you are still under oath." "Yes, your Honor."

"Ms. Thompson where were you the night of Mr. Tunnel's emergency?" "I had just finished surgery and was trying to get something to eat, when my pager went off." "I thought you said he usually has five working with him during surgery?" "Yes, he does but for some reason he wanted six of us for this surgery." (This was the one thing Sam did not have and I was about to tell him. It will complete his puzzle.) Sam just looked at her with his mouth opened. "Why wasn't your name on the sign in sheet?" "Well, since I was called in at the last minute, I didn't have time to run to the sign in sheet." "Mr. Tunnel was already in the operating room." "I figured Dr. Sampson would do that when he completed his records and he never asked me if I signed the sheet."

"Could you tell us what happened in the operating room." "Your Honor, we already heard from four previous nurses on this subject." "Yes, I know." "Mr. Carlson, where are you going with this line of questioning when we heard from the other nurses," "Well your Honor, if I can have some lead way, it will make sense." "Alright, however get to your point." "Yes your Honor."

"Okay Ms. Thompson, please tell us in your exact words what happened." "Well, we proceeded to prepare Mr. Tunnel for his procedure and when the anesthesiologist stated Mr. Tunnel was ready, Dr Sampson picked up the saw you use to cut the chest cavity open, however when he started he used the same incision he used for the first operation." "This incision was not really strong enough for that kind of opening and when he did that he lost control of the saw because the scare was still tender and it went into his heart and cut it." The courtroom gasped.

"You mean, he cut the heart?" "Yes" Jane started crying. "What happened next." "Well Mr. Tunnel, died instantly." "There was no way he could repair that."

Mr. Locker threw down his pencil and just sat there and looked at Dr. Sampson. Dr. Sampson put his head down.

"What happened next?" "Dr. Sampson asked us to stop what we were doing and told us that what happened here would remain here and we were not to speak about it outside this operating room." "Did you tell any other nurses who were not in surgery with you that night." "No" "He made us swear to secrecy." "Dr. Sampson, stated if this was talked about at anytime outside the OR we would loose our jobs." "You mean he threatened you." "Yes sir, he was Chief of Cardiology Surgery, he could do anything he wanted." "I was fearful for my job, I didn't want to loose it." "I was making good money and I really liked working at that hospital." "I knew if I spoke up I wouldn't get a job anywhere, he would of made sure of that." "So why are you speaking up now." "Well when I heard that this case was being reopened, I couldn't live with myself any more." "I had to speak up." Jane started crying again. "It just wasn't right that anyone should do that and get away with it." She looked at Mrs. Tunnel and mouthed I'm sorry. Sam put his arm around Mrs. Tunnel and squeezed her, leaned over to her and said "We Won."

"Thank you Ms. Thompson."

"Any questions Mr. Locker?" He stood up and said "No your Honor, none."

As each nurse was recalled they all stated the same story and stated they received the same threat. It was obvious with their testimony he had no chance of getting a not guilty verdict."

The judge seemed horrified however she couldn't really say anything. "Your Honor the plaintiff rest."

"Does the defense have anyone to recall." "No your Honor the defense rests also." "Okay court is dismissed for the day." "I will give this to the jury tomorrow."

Chapter 47

S am and Kerry stood up and hugged each other. "Where in the world did that come from?" "Well I must confess, Jane came to me a few weeks ago and told me the entire story." "Why didn't you say anything." "To tell you the truth I didn't know how you would react since it was Jane and Jane was so upset, so I decided to just wait till trial."

Sam couldn't talk to Jane until after the verdict came back, he wanted to say something to her so bad but knew he couldn't, not yet.

The next day they were back in court where the judge explained the decision the jury had to make. She explained that they had first to decide whether their was negligence on the part of the doctor or wrongful death. Then if they decided the defendant was guilty they had to decide as to whether there was enough to pay punitive damages to the plaintiff. If they did they also had to decide as to whether they would compensate Mrs. Tunnel for the death of her husband.

Sam and Kerry went back to the office to settle in for the duration of the day and wait for the call. "You know Kerry, we make great partners. We should combine our offices and make a partnership." "You know Sam, I was hoping you would say that, because I really would like to do that." "Okay, sounds good, we can think of a name after the verdict." "I personally think our partnership can be made on a handshake." "What do you think?" Kerry stood up and said "I agree."

They both were on pins and needles so they decided to call Frank and get some lunch. "Frank, this is Kerry, the jury is out and we thought you would like to have lunch with us while we are waiting for the call." "You said you wanted to be there for the verdict also, so if we get the call we can all go back to the courtroom together." "Sounds great." "I'll met you at Harry's."

Kerry got off the phone and asked Sam what's Harry's? "Only the best bar and grill this side of Chicago." "They got the best steaks there." "Well how come I'm just finding out about this now." "Well I guess we've been busy." "Yea, it sounds like you two have been keeping a big delicious secret from number three." "Come on, let's go and have a great lunch, which I think will be having many together from now on."

They arrived at Harry's and it was filled. "Somehow they managed to get a table for the three of them. As they sat down, Frank said, "I understand you had a great day yesterday?" "Yea we sure did and because of that day, today Kerry and I decided to join our offices and become partners." "I knew that would happened, it was just a matter of time." "Congratulations." "Don't know what we will call ourselves, that is something we can think of later." "Hey Sam, I have a great Private Investigator we could hire also." "Gee I wonder who that could be." "Kerry if you marry this girl are you going to be able to work side by side at our office" "I don't think that will ever be a problem." "Well, after we are settled in you can approach her on the idea."

About two hours into their long lunch, Sam's phone started ringing. Then Kerry's phone started ringing. They both looked at each other and said "The jury's back."

"Well now, I'm nauseated." Sam said, "Come on Sam, keep the faith man, we got this." "Okay, Kerry you don't know how bad I have wanted this win for Mrs. Tunnel." "I do and you will get your win." "Here comes that nonchalant personality out again." "Well someone has to be that way if we are going to be partners."

s everyone filed in, so did the press. Some how the word spread like wild fire what happened in the court room yesterday. Every seat was filled.

Dr. Sampson walked down the isle and looked sick when he sat down with his attorneys. Kerry leaned over to Sam and said "Look at him, he must have gotten a ripping from his attorneys at lunch." "Yea, that is if he could eat." "Well he has a lot of problems coming up." "Yea, he don't know the half of them yet."

As the jury filed in, they looked like the wind was kicked out of them. Sam and Kerry were surprised when they saw them. Neither of them ever saw a jury come in looking like that.

The judge came in and stated "Mr. Foreman, have you reached a verdict." "We have your Honor." "What is your verdict?" "We the jury find Dr. Sampson guilty. The courtroom made some quite cheering. "Silence, please no noise until after we read the entire verdict."

"On Punitive damages we award Mrs. Tunnel (Sam put his hand in hers and held it tight) in the amount of $50 million dollars. (Sam's mouth dropped) and on Compensatory damages we award the plaintiff $100 million dollars. Kerry leaned over to Sam and said "I think you just made history in Chicago." Sam couldn't say a thing, he just nodded his head.

"Your Honor the jury would like to make a special request." "Yes" "We request that Dr. Sampson's license be revoked for a total of 10 years also." "Well, unfortunately that is not in your right to make that decision but I will pass this information on to the Medical Board." "I will say that this trial has been very difficult for everyone involved and with this case we must make aware to the medical field to have stricter guidelines when it comes to our patients and physicians." "They need to be held accountable for the procedures and operations that take place in our hospitals and the hospitals need to be vigilante on judging mistakes that are made."

"If there is nothing else, case dismissed." "Sam stood up and wrapped his arms around Mrs. Tunnel "You won, you won."

Mrs. Tunnel started to cry. "Sam I don't know what to say." "Don't say anything, just take your money, you have been awarded and make a good life for you and your two children." "Your husband would have wanted you to do that." "You deserve that." "I'll call you later next week and we can go over the details of what just happened here." "Okay Sam." "Thank you so very much." "Your welcome." "Now go and get your kids and be with your family." Sam and Kerry just stood there and watched her walk down the isle. "Kerry I am so happy for her." "Yea I'm happy for you." "But I told you have the faith."

Chapter 49

"**A**s they were standing there watching her. there was a commotion at the back of the courtroom. Sam and Kerry forgot that Frank was standing at the back of the courtroom during the decision. As Dr. Sampson approached Frank he stopped him. He said "Dr. Sampson I am Detective Frank Young of the Chicago Police Department." "You my friend are under arrest for drug trafficking. "We've been watching your two little rentals for quite awhile now." "You certainly get a lot of delivery packages don't you?" "Your friends are already downtown." "I think their spilling their guts and cutting a deal." "So you better think about what you will be saying when we get down there." "This is ridiculous., you have nothing on me." "I can't wait to hear about your exciting trip to the Bahama's." "I heard it was nice." "Now turn around" Frank slapped the cuffs on him. "We might even be able to get involuntary manslaughter out of this also." "At least we'll try."

*

As he was walking out, Sam and Kerry could here Frank reading Dr. Sampson his rights. "Charlie, take him downtown and book him." Sam said. "Well Frank you told me if I ever had anything. to throw it your way." "I did, and you through me a big fish." "The city of Chicago thanks you." Frank will be enjoying this for quite awhile.

Chapter 50

As Sam and Kerry were standing there Frank walked up to them. "Well Sam, which one is Jane?" "Jane come over here." "Sam I am so sorry." "Jane don't worry about it." "Everything is fine." "I totally understand." "Frank, I want you to meet Jane." "Ahhh, so this was your secret weapon Kerry." ""Yes this is Jane." "Nice to finally meet you, Kerry told me about you." "Jane this is the guy Kerry took your information to." "Frank I am so happy to finally meet you." "Sam has taked about you so often." "Boy I am so glad that this is over." "Jane, Frank is my other oldest and dearest friend. "Frank said "Jane your friend did a lot of leg work for us." "He's a great guy and should think about being a policeman." "I will, I'll deliver the message." "Thank you."

"Did you know you helped us bring down the largest drug trafficking ring in the city of Chicago area?" "The city of Chicago thanks you." "Your welcome Frank and nice to meet you."

The next day Kerry called Sam. "Sam did you see the paper yet?" "Yea Phyliss just handed it to me." "I like the headline." The Chicago Tribune hit the stands with headline news. The headline read. Yesterday. Largest medical malpractice case in the history of Illinois settles for $150 million dollars." "I like

that headline, we need to frame that when we join forces."
"Okay I want to read this article. I'll call you later Kerry."

The article went on to say the doctor worked at Greyson Medical Center. The particulars of the case are being withheld to protect the privacy of the family.

This case has created a storm of anger with people that feel doctors are not taking it seriously enough in telling the truth on errors on patients as important as they should.

This hopefully will make doctors aware of how important a life is and hospitals will take more time to investigate medical mistakes.

Lets see, I win my case and make headlines, Mrs. Tunnel wins and is finally at peace with the truth and will be able to take care of her two children without worrying about money ever again. Got a drug trafficker off the streets which made Frank happy and Dr. Sampson will be going to jail. Kerry and I are going into partnership together and I'll be getting married. I'd say this was a great 6 months Life is looking great.

About the Author

Pam Bridy lives in Harrisburg Pennsylvania. She attended a two year medical assistant school and did a rotation in the city at Baltimore Hospital. She is retired now and worked in the medical field for forty years. She has two children and five grandchildren. While working in the medical field for so long she decided to write a book about issues in the medical field and what can go wrong.